MISTRESS MURDER

A Sixties Mystery

BERNARD KNIGHT

First published in Great Britain by Robert Hale Ltd 1966
This edition published by Accent Press 2015

ISBN 9781910939970

Copyright © Bernard Knight 1966, 2015

The right of Bernard Knight to be identified as the author
of this work has been asserted by the author in accordance
with the Copyright, Designs and Patents Act 1988.

To Jean –
my wife and most constant critic

Author's Note

The Sixties Mysteries is a series of reissues of my early crime stories, the first of which was originally published in 1963. Looking back now, it is evident how criminal investigation has changed over the last half-century. Though basic police procedure is broadly the same, in these pages you will find no Crime Scene Managers or Crown Prosecution Service, no DNA, CSI, PACE, nor any of the other acronyms beloved of modern novels and television. These were the days when detectives still wore belted raincoats and trilby hats. There was no Health and Safety to plague us and the police smoked and drank tea alongside the post-mortem table!

Modern juries are now more interested in the reports of the forensic laboratory than in the diligent labours of the humble detective, though it is still the latter that solves most serious crimes. This is not to by any means belittle the enormous advances made in forensic science in recent years, but to serve as a reminder that the old murder teams did a pretty good job based simply on experience and dogged investigation.

Bernard Knight
2015

Chapter One

Paul Jacobs walked sedately up from the subway of Cardiff railway station and paused on platform one to consult his wristwatch.

The waiting London-bound diesel had three minutes to go. He gave a little satisfied smirk at his impeccable timing then climbed aboard to claim his reserved seat in a First Class compartment.

Jacobs put his expensive suitcase on the rack and fiddled with it until it sat exactly right. Then with a deliberation that made the passenger opposite want to scream with exasperation, he neatly folded his light overcoat, placed it immaculately on the case and finally, with the air of a master conjurer at the climax of his act, crowned the lot with his black homburg. He turned and nodded briefly at the other two businessmen who shared the compartment and sat down.

The fellow opposite, the one who was growing the duodenal ulcer, swallowed his nerves and gave him the quick meaningless smile that un-introduced first class travellers use, then dived back into his *Western Mail*. Paul Jacobs shook out a pink *Financial Times* as the diesel rolled slowly out of the station, dead on eleven twenty-six.

For an hour, the three gentlemen sat in a silence as holy as that of the British Museum. Then Jacobs got up and followed the steward's advice about first lunch.

He had a good meal in the restaurant car, enjoyed a brandy and a cigar then came back to his seat for the rest of the journey to Paddington.

If either of his travelling companions had been asked

on oath to say what they remembered about him, probably the only thing that would have stuck in their minds was the fact that the magazine that he took out after lunch was in German. Otherwise they would have had to describe him – to the despair of the police – as 'of average height – medium build, brown hair – or was it rather fair? Oh yes, he wore glasses.'

A woman might have done better, for she might have thought him as definitely fair with a high forehead and quite good-looking.

This anonymity of appearance was part of Jacob's professional stock-in-trade. It helped him to keep his income in the six-figure range. But none of this was ever to be put to his fellow travellers. He read his German magazine undisturbed until they reached Paddington. Then he took down his case, made farewell smiles at them and stepped onto the platform.

Jacobs walked leisurely down the platform, across the crowded area at the top and back down to the toilets on platform one. There, in the cramped but complete privacy of a cubicle, he shed his carefully assumed role of a sedate provincial businessman. Paul Jacobs went into storage in the suitcase. His dark overcoat, briefcase and umbrella were stowed away. He took everything from the pockets of his grey suit – everything that his wife expected him to carry: diary, letters, wallet, keys – they all went into the suitcase. All he kept was some loose change and a wad of banknotes. The last things to go were his heavy-rimmed spectacles, the lenses of which were almost plain glass.

He snapped the case shut with a satisfied click and walked back up the platform to the Left Luggage Office. There he exchanged the identity of Paul Jacobs for a pink ticket and called a taxi at the rank.

For the next ten minutes, he was in a personal no-man's-land as the taxi took him across London to Euston, but at the other station he reversed the process with a ticket carefully retrieved from the bottom of his breast pocket.

He took the new case, a large and ostentatious lightweight, to the nearest gents' and extracted from it the personality of Paul Golding. He put on a cream-coloured waterproof overcoat of an expensively rakish cut, fitted another wallet and diary into his pockets, and took out some more keys and a few papers. Finally, he put on an American-looking pork pie hat with a wide band and changed his shoes for grey suede with elastic sides.

When he stepped out of the lavatory a few moments later, swinging the empty case, he was an utterly different man from the one who had arrived at Paddington half an hour earlier. Though he had no false beard or cheek pads, his golf and business acquaintances in Cardiff would have passed him in the street without a second glance.

The second taxi took him to a block of flats in Newman Street, literally within a stone's throw of the edge of Soho. As he stood paying off the driver, he could see the top end of Dean Street beyond the milling traffic in Oxford Street. Paul had picked this place with great care. As he went into the entrance hall, there was no curious porter to mark his comings and goings; the lift that whisked him up to the fourth floor had no gossiping attendant, only a row of buttons.

He reached his flat and let himself in with a key from the Euston suitcase.

'Paul? Paul, is that you, darling?'

A woman's voice came from the room on the left of the tiny hallway. As he pushed the door open, she ran towards him across the carpet, barefoot, her arms wide open. Now she was in his arms, her hands on his neck and her lips burrowing into his. Paul felt the warmth flowing through him as she strained against his chest. Her mouth moved excitingly and sensually on his, but, as he gave himself up to enjoyment, a part of his mind stayed detached. It was comparing her kisses with those of his wife, now probably playing bridge with her friends in a Cardiff suburb. He decided that if Barbara practised for twenty years she could never kiss like Rita. Eventually his mistress pulled away and leant back, holding on to his hands, looking like a sleek cat after some long overdue cream.

'Paul, you're three days later this time – over a fortnight.'

She pouted delightfully, her lips quivering, ready for more.

'Miss me, sweet?'

'Of course – I always do.'

'I expect you found something to do, beautiful.'

'What is there to do?' Her voice had a foreign huskiness.

'Come and sit down, we can't stand up all the time.'

A little warning bell rang in his mind. His exquisite sense of self-preservation hovered over her words. Had there been a little hesitation there – was she covering up?

'What have you been doing, anyway?' he asked as they moved to the settee.

'Same damn things,' she pouted. 'Hairdressers, a couple of shows … what else is there to do when you stay away so long?'

Nothing there, he thought. His early warning system stopped buzzing, but stayed watchful. Rita pulled him to her on the settee, the focal point of the small but beautifully furnished lounge. She tossed back her hair carelessly and slid her arms around his neck. He pressed his face against her hair, which was as genuinely black as her fiery Italian blood.

'Kiss me again, Paul … two whole weeks, you swine!'

As he obliged, he wondered whether she was overdoing this 'happy return' routine. With the print of her lips fresh on his, he rebelled at the need to be suspicious, but his cautious mind told him to get to his secret box in the bedroom as soon as he could. They kissed again, the

4

woman's enthusiasm lulling his doubts. When they drew apart, he sank back against the cushions and looked her over. His brows came together in a frown.

'Why d'you wear those damn trousers, sweet ... you know I can't stand them?'

She looked down at her long legs sheathed in skin-tight jeans.

'Sorry – but I didn't know you were going to come today, did I?'

She looked at him with her dark spaniel eyes and he laughed.

'OK, I'm not going to leather you this time – come here.'

They went into another passionate clinch. After a decent interval, Rita broke away and jumped up.

'I must be getting old – I can't hold my breath that long!'

She laughed gaily and stretched luxuriously in front of him. Was she breaking it off sooner than usual? He cursed his suspicious mind and reached forwards to grip her round the waist.

'What about changing out of these abominations?' He pinched her through her tights.

'Aoww ... swine!' She bent down and bit him hard on the ear. Before he could retaliate, she had skipped away to the door of the bedroom.

'I've got to have my hair done at four, so I'll have to change anyway.'

She vanished and Paul sat brooding for a few seconds. She's going out – good! A chance to have a look in the box. He got up quickly.

'I'll come and help you change.'

Moving fast he reached the bedroom door before she could slam it and lean against the other side.

He grinned, pushed it open with his shoulder and chased her round the big bed. She ran squealing with delight, barefoot over the coverlet, but let herself be caught without much trouble. He brought her down with a thump on to the bed.

'I've told you before not to wear these when I come home.'

His hands were busy at the waistband of her jeans and she was kissing him again.

'Hairdresser's by four, darling!' she whispered practically.

Paul listened at the door until he heard the whine of the lift taking her down.

'She should be gone a good hour and a half,' he muttered as he took a beer from the refrigerator. He spent ten minutes over it to make sure she didn't come back for some reason, then got down to business.

He went to a drawer and took out a screwdriver. Going into the bedroom, he knelt in front of a built-in wardrobe and pulled the doors open. Parting a row of expensive dresses, he cleared the floor of shoes and hatboxes to expose the boards. Taking out six screws, Paul lifted the floor out entirely and laid it on the carpet. The cavity beneath was lined with a thick layer of sound-proofing sponge. In the centre was a tape recorder with unusually large spools. Fine wires led from it to the back of the nearby skirting board, where the junction box of the bedside telephone was fixed.

Paul looked at the amount of tape that had passed on to the take-up spool. He frowned and the cold part of his brain said, 'I told you so!'

On previous occasions when he had come to his 'bugging' apparatus, there had been hardly any tape used at all. This time, well over half of the big spool had passed over and as he pressed the rewind button, he felt already resigned to the inevitable. This had to happen sooner or later, he thought regretfully.

Paul Jacobs picked up a little earpiece and thrust it in

place. With a sigh, he pressed the playback button.

That evening, he took Rita to the Nineties Club, in Gerrard Street, on the side of Soho furthest from their flat.

In spite of the revelation of the tape recorder, Paul's manner towards his mistress was the same – a mixture of affection and domination. In turn, Rita showed her usual vivacity and coquettishness. She had no idea that he had heard every word of her telephone conversations for the past fortnight.

He helped her out of a taxi in front of the Nineties at about nine thirty. They walked to the door, sandwiched between a brash amusement arcade and a smart Chinese restaurant.

'Evening, Mr Golding.'

The doorman, his physique suggesting his real function of bouncer, saluted them smartly. They passed through the narrow doorway under the neon Can-Can sign that flickered over the entrance.

The uninspiring exterior of the place gave way to an imaginative and expensive decor. The club proper was in the basement and they walked down a heavily-carpeted stairway to reach it. The walls were hung with Victorian draperies with many heavily ornamented mirrors. There were framed theatre posters from the last years of the old century, to set the atmosphere that gave the club its name. Even the chucker-out doorman wore a top hat and side whiskers to mimic the 'good old days'

At the bottom of the stairs was a small cloakroom with an attractive girl to take Paul's coat and Rita's mink cape. Paul wore a dinner jacket and Rita a slinky cocktail dress. She looked very different from the sweater and jeans of the afternoon, but even more alluring.

Jacobs looked at her back with regret as he followed her through the padded swing-doors into the club itself. This was a long room which extended the whole length of the building above. At the further end was a small stage for the band and cabaret, and along the left-hand wall was a long and ornate bar. Paul shepherded his mistress towards it and found a couple of high stools still vacant.

The barman hurried up, his leathery face crinkled in smiles.

'Mr Golding ... Miss Ronalde ... nice to see you!'

He sounded as if he really meant it.

'The usual, Snigger,' replied Golding. 'Brandy ginger for Rita, gin and French for me.'

The barman bustled off to get the drinks. He had two barmaids and a waiter to assist him, but he dealt with this order himself. He was a little man, who looked like an ex-jockey, mainly because he was an ex-jockey – ex because he had been caught doping his competitor's steeds a few years before.

He came back with the drinks and waved away Paul's offer to pay.

'First one's on me, as usual, Mr Golding.'

'Everything all right, Snigger?' asked Paul.

There was more in the casual remark than anyone other than themselves realised.

Snigger winked and gave a thumbs-up sign.

'Fine ... same with you?'

Golding nodded shortly, but the barman recognised the lack of conviction. A barmaid came up to him with some query and he moved away down the bar.

Rita was looking around the room, which was almost full to capacity – a typical Saturday night crowd. She tried to make her inspection look like idle curiosity, but Paul knew that she was hoping to catch a glimpse of someone special – the other voice on the tape.

'Ready for another?'

His voice jerked her attention back to the bar and she gave him a bright, but mechanical, smile.

'Mmm, please, same again.'

She finished her drink quickly, gave him another dazzling smile and slid her arm through his.

He smiled back, patted her arm and said, 'Bitch,' to himself. She prattled on about nothing in particular, making the sweet talk that he had enjoyed, along with her Latin-style lovemaking, for the past eighteen months – since he had picked her up in this very bar, in fact.

But, more sensitive than ever tonight, he noticed that, even as she talked, her eyes kept straying to the big mirrors behind the bar, searching the reflection of the people in the crowded room.

The bar and the rest of the club repeated the late Victorian motif of the entrance. The barman wore the striped shirt, collar, cravat, and armbands of the period, and even had a pair of false side-whiskers and moustache. His attractive barmaids were dressed in bustled full-skirted dresses with alarmingly low necklines. The draperies and bar fitments were all authentic and the huge ornamented mirrors which Rita found so interesting were from a demolished London pub of the eighteen-eighties.

Snigger was still busy down the bar and his assistant, an adenoidal man dressed in a similar outfit, fixed their second drinks. After a few minutes, Paul casually excused himself and strolled in the direction of the toilets, which played such a big part in his double life. As he passed the lower end of the bar, he gave Snigger an almost imperceptible jerk of the head. The barman responded by raising his eyebrows a sixteenth of an inch and after a moment or two, followed him out.

They met in the washroom and waited until another man left. Then they stood washing their hands unnecessarily at adjacent basins while they talked.

'How's tricks?' asked the ex-jockey.

'Bloody awful – but don't worry, it's nothing to do with – the racket.'

Snigger allowed his George Robey eyebrows another

excursion up his forehead, but said nothing. He knew better than to push his curiosity with Paul Golding.

'Going over tomorrow?' he asked instead.

'Yes, Brussels this time. How much do you want?' Snigger, his name an obvious parody on his unfortunate real one of Leonard Gigal, looked cautiously over his shoulder to see if the door was shut. Heroin … as much as you like. That last lot of morphine you dumped on me will take months to get rid of.'

Paul nodded. He straightened his back and pulled the plug out of the basin.

'Right – can you take five hundred grams?'

The barman whistled.

'Five hundred! OK, I'll take it. They all seem to be after the hard stuff these days … it may take a few weeks to palm off, mind.'

Paul nodded and went to dry his hands at a roller towel. 'I'll be back on Thursday … come up Friday night for it, usual place.'

Gigal looked curiously at the other man. Golding was affable, but drew a strict line about the limits of his confidence in people. Snigger tried again, tentatively.

'How you going this time, Rotterdam routine again?' Paul looked hard at him, his jaw muscles tensing.

'No, I'm not,' he said harshly. 'The less you know, the less you can spill when you get picked up.'

Snigger smiled weakly. He accepted the brush-off and the hint that the Metropolitan Police would catch up with him sooner or later. The innuendo that when he was nicked he would do well to keep his mouth shut was not lost on him either. He decided to change the subject.

'Rita's looking smashing tonight – smartest bird that comes in here.' He grinned ingratiatingly, showing his loose oversize dentures.

'Shut up – let's get out of here. Folks'll wonder what we're up to.'

Just outside the toilet, Paul stopped in the shadow of a supporting pillar and looked towards the bar. Rita was still on her stool, openly searching the club with her eyes. Paul waited a moment to see if she had any success. The tape recorder had given him the sound of the other man's voice, but it had not been one he recognised. And, infuriatingly, never once had either he or Rita spoken his name, not even the Christian name. Paul remembered the endearments – and worse – that had passed between them.

He felt no jealousy, only annoyance at the enforced break-up of a carnally satisfactory arrangement. But more serious, there was the anxiety about the safety of his identity and his drug smuggling business.

He saw no sign that Rita had recognised anyone and he made his way back to her.

'Shall we dance?' he said.

They spent the rest of the time until the 11.30 cabaret, clinging together on the tiny floor, swaying to the smooch music of the four-piece band. There was no twisting or shaking here. This was strictly a hideout for the tired and not-so-tired business man who wanted to get to grips with his social life in the shape of a young woman.

There was nothing about the place that would attract the attention of the Yard Vice Squad, but an unaccompanied tired businessman had only to cross Snigger's palm with a fiver for an attractive girl to appear within five minutes, to be his drinking and dancing partner. What she chose to do when the club closed at two thirty was her own business, as far as the club was concerned.

Half an hour before midnight, the already dim lights went down even further and a blue spotlight appeared on the stage. For the first time, the club owner appeared, his shirt front glowing in the eerie light. There was a desultory burst of applause and he held his hands up for silence.

Snigger snorted from behind the bar where he was

polishing a glass.

'Think he was going to conduct Beethoven's *Fiff* in the Albert 'All!' he growled in his broad Cockney. 'One night I'm going to wrap a bottle round his bleeding 'ead!'

Paul Jacobs' bland face stared hard at the barman. 'It would cost you some if you did, Snigger,' he said enigmatically. He turned back to the stage. Ray Silver, a plump Eurasian and owner of the club, was giving a build-up patter for the cabaret.

All the acts had changed since Paul's last visit a few weeks before and he listened to the new artistes with interest. The third and last performer riveted his attention even more firmly.

Ray Silver bounced on to announce Fraulein Elsa and amid a roll of drums, a tall blonde drifted on to the stage. The cloud of silver hair was accentuated by the harsh blue light as she sung 'Lili Marlene' huskily and sensually in the style of the ageless German-American star, Marlene Dietrich. Her voice alone would never have made her fortune, thought Paul as he carefully looked her over, but the meaning she put into the words and the way she moved her long body inside the glittering sheath of her dress more than made up for an indifferent set of vocal cords.

Elsa followed 'Lili Marlene' with a couple of even more glowing numbers from Eartha Kitt's repertoire. Paul's attention was so rapt that his usually steel-willed caution slipped for a few minutes.

His eyes, focussed on the swaying silver figure, failed to notice Rita making furtive signs to a man who had just come through the swing doors. The man stood, as Jacobs had done, in the shadow of a pillar, staring intently at the pair at the bar.

Behind Paul's back, Rita made a little warning motion with her cigarette, pointing fleetingly at her escort. The stranger, a tall, broad man in his early thirties, gave a slight nod. Then he went to the other end of the bar and completely ignored the other pair for the rest of the night.

Paul watched the Austrian singer intently until the end of her act. Already the germ of an idea as to Rita's successor was taking root in his calculating mind. When she left the stage in a burst of applause Rita left to powder her nose. Paul swung back to the bar and called Snigger for some more drinks.

Gigal leered at him.

'Nice bit 'o stuff, eh? The "frowline" stunt is on the level too – she really does come from Vienna.'

'Know anything about her?'

The little cockney shrugged. 'She's only been here a week. No bloke hanging around her yet, if that's what you mean.'

'Where's she live?'

Again Snigger shrugged. 'Search me! I'll put the whisper around, if you like.'

Paul nodded then leant forwards across the bar.

'Snigger, have you noticed anyone hanging around Rita this last couple of weeks?' He dropped his voice as he spoke.

The ex-jockey's brows went up again.

'A feller? No, she ain't even bin in here ... no, wait a bit, she was once. But on her own, she was. Straight up, that is.'

Paul accepted his word and let the subject drop. He slid off the stool and stubbed his cigarette out.

'I'm going in to see Silver for a minute. Tell Rita I won't be long.'

The barman, looking incongruous in his whiskers and armbands, nodded. 'Want me to keep my eyes skinned when you're away?' he offered tentatively.

Paul scowled at him. 'Don't bother ... I'm taking care of it.'

Snigger shied off the delicate ground of Golding's personal affairs. Theirs was a purely business relationship.

The ex-jockey was a middleman in the dope business in the West End. He bought the stuff wholesale from Golding, broke it down into smaller packages and sold it at a handsome profit to the dealers.

They had a series of safeguards which made it virtually impossible for the police to trace the supply back to Golding. For eight years now they had carried on this rewarding game without a whisper of trouble. Snigger knew that he was by no means the only distributor for Golding's imports from the Continent. Ray Silver was another, for instance.

He was a big-time middleman and through his interests in a chain of seedy dance halls through London, he got rid of a much larger quantity than Snigger himself. Silver dealt mainly with teenage pep pills and reefers, but had a fair trade in the hard stuff: heroin, morphine, and cocaine. Snigger also knew that Paul's visit now to the office at the back of the stage was to take Silver's order for the next consignment from Brussels.

Golding left the bar just before Rita came back, her curvaceous body sidling between the crowded tables. The barman looked covertly at her as she approached and wondered what had made Golding suspect that she was two-timing him.

'You're soon going to get your cards and week's money, sweetheart,' he muttered to himself as the dark beauty pirouetted onto her stool.

He leant back against his mirrored shelves and looked around the big room, now thick with cigarette smoke. His two full-bosomed assistants were serving as fast as they could go, and Albert, the waiter, rushed around the tables, his speed in serving varying with the expected size of his tip. He was a small cog in the drug market, being one of Silver's distributors. Under cover of serving drinks, he would pass over packets of dope, the profits largely going to the club owner. Silver had no idea that his barman was a competitor under his own roof. Albert had a shrewd idea how Snigger passed his stuff across, but the barman paid him a regular sub to keep his mouth shut.

Snigger leisurely polished an already gleaming glass as he looked around the big room, now full of chattering voices, the drone of the band and the click of fruit machines from the other corner. He looked up and down the bar – every stool except Golding's being occupied. Amongst the line of tired businessmen, he noticed an M.P., a couple of stage and TV people, and a sprinkling of showgirls and strippers. The Nineties was no club for the mugs and tourists who crowded into Soho – it existed for the hard core of the West End population, a place where business and vice rubbed shoulders with sophisticated pleasure.

His eye passed from a couple of attractive chorus girls to the man next to them. He recognised him as Conrad Draper, a big-time bookie who had benefited from many hundreds of pounds of Snigger's money in past years.

Like Gigal himself, Conrad was a product of the East End. He had catapulted to affluence and dubious fame about three years ago. Before that, he had been a wrestler and a strong-arm man for several unsavoury gentlemen of the turf. By means of some smart takeover bids, together with a deal of physical intimidation, he had rapidly ousted many of the smaller bookmakers and built up a monopoly of betting shops in Soho and the back streets of the West End. He had a finger in the protection rackets of the area and he was doing his best to become the Al Capone of Central London.

Snigger watched him out of the corner of his eye as he sat idly twisting a whisky glass in his fingers. He had a large unlit cigar in his mouth. It fascinated the barman to see him take it out occasionally, lay it carefully on the edge of the ashtray, and take out a cigarette to smoke. After a few draws, he would crush it out and put the cigar back between his fleshy lips. He was a good six foot two in height and had the shoulders of a wrestler, as well as the experience. He was handsome in a heavy sort of way, but his features were already thickening and he had a slightly bent nose as a legacy of his days in the ring. Since he had got near the top of the Soho mobsters, he affected an American drawl and style of dress. He wore a flashy blue drape suit with narrow lapels and was liberally decked out with tiepins and signet rings. In the cloakroom hung an expensive camel-hair coat and a wide-brimmed Chicago-style hat.

Paul came back from his business with the club owner and disturbed Snigger's browsing by asking for more drinks. Rita and he sat talking while they finished them then went off to the dance floor.

After a few more smoochy dances, the couple came back to the bar. Rita had drunk quite a lot in the course of the evening and was getting sentimentally tipsy. She lolled against Paul a little too obviously and began stroking his sleeve. He frowned and gently pushed her upright.

'Come on – time for bed ... you're getting high.'

It was a quirk of his dual personality that in spite of his organised adultery, his immoral drug dealings and his crooked friend, he still had a wide streak of prudery which rebelled against seeing her drunk in public.

Rita giggled and tried to kiss him. He scowled, drew away, then his face cleared. The first glimmerings of a plan for her elimination came to him at that instant. He stood up, slid an arm around her bare shoulders and aimed her towards the door.

'You've had enough for tonight, gorgeous,' he murmured gently. He piloted her to the cloakroom and got their things from the girl. He slipped the mink around her, reflecting that it had cost him the whole proceeds of a trip to Marseilles the year before. He steered her up the stairs and the pugilistic doorman called a cab.

While they waited, she buried her face in his chest. 'I want to kiss you, darling,' she pouted tipsily.

He smiled grimly above her head into the neon jungle of Soho. 'You can kiss me all you like, once we get home,' he promised.

He added silently, 'And you can kiss him tomorrow, Rita, as arranged ... make the most of it!'

Chapter Two

Paul Jacobs had plenty of time for reflection and planning on the following day.

He made his usual cover-up visit to a silver vault in St. Martin's Lane in the morning and made purchases worth a few hundred pounds. For the short time that he was in the vaults, he partly reverted to his Paul Jacobs identity, having left his fancy hat and coat in the flat. He paid by cheque drawn on a legitimate account in Cardiff and arranged for the silver to be insured and delivered to his antique business in Cardiff's dockland.

Having finished this genuine excuse for spending the better part of a week in London, he went back to Newman Street. He packed a case, took some documents and money from a wall safe and kissed Rita goodbye.

She had learned to show no curiosity about either his business affairs or his erratic comings and goings. Clinging to his arm, she went with him to the lift.

'See you on Saturday, sweet,' he said, as he stepped inside. 'We'll have a special night, eh? Be good till then!'

He smiled grimly as he went down to the foyer. He knew the sort of goodness she would be indulging in with her new boyfriend the moment he was gone.

At the top of the shaft she stood looking down, her mind filled with her own private thoughts.

'Going to Glasgow, be damned! I wonder which passport he's using this time.'

As she went back into the bedroom and picked up the telephone, Paul was walking to a nearby lock-up garage to take out his Jaguar.

After an hour's difficult driving to get clear of Greater London, he got the grey Mark X onto the motorway and put his foot down for Dover. The big car slid quietly along in the outer lane with the needle steadily hovering on the ninety mark. The traffic was light on this dull November day and he could let his thoughts wander around his immediate problems.

He blessed the foresight which had prompted him some six months before to hook up the tape recorder to his telephone. At the time, he had no reason to suspect Rita of any double dealing, but the idea had come to him and his razor-edged sense of self-preservation had made him act on .it. For five and a half of those months, the spools had picked up nothing suspicious. He supposed that unless the affair between Rita and Mr X had been a whirlwind romance, the first stages had gone somewhere outside the flat – especially as the conversations on the tape had started abruptly on a most intimate level.

He could still hear them now, as if the recorder were inside his head.

'Darling – how are you feeling this morning?' – meaningful sniggers – 'Look, you shouldn't ring me here.'

'Why not? You told me he's not back for a week.'

'Well, he usually only comes about once a fortnight – but you never know.'

'Oh, to hell with him!' More nauseating giggles and *innuendos about the previous night.*

'But we mustn't get careless, honey ... and I'm coming round tomorrow – only until Saturday, we mustn't risk leaving it till later, he's due anytime after that.'

There followed several feet of tape that caused Paul no jealousy, but intense annoyance to think that the woman had been using his bed, clothes, and telephone to carry on with another man.

Then the important business began.

'Look, honey, I rang you for something special,' said

the unidentifiable voice. 'If it comes off, it won't matter a damn about him finding out about us – he'll have too much else to worry about.'

'What are you on about, for God's sake?'

'This sugar daddy of yours – Golding. Know who he is?'

The rough East End voice with a thin veneer of Americanised club drawl held an expectant note of triumph.

'No, why should I?' answered the girl. 'He always brushes me off when I get nosy – so now I don't. I suppose he's some well-heeled business man from out of town, with a wife and kids – he naturally wants to keep me well out of his private life.'

'So you don't know.'

The man's voice kept the suspense up and Rita became ratty.

'Look, lover, cut the mystery will you? What are you trying to say?'

'Sweetie, have you any idea what his business is?' The sham cultured overlay in the man's voice cracked under the strain of his excitement.

'No, I bloody well haven't – he can sell ladies' underwear for all I care, as long as he keeps me in nylons and mink.'

'Gorgeous, your boyfriend is a big-time dope peddler!'

The unknown voice, exasperatingly unknown to Golding, reached an exultant peak.

Rita was incredulous, but the voice went on to explain that one of his boys had recognised him in the Nineties Club the week before. This boy had once been pushing drugs himself and had dealt with Golding as a supplier. Paul cursed – this was a loophole that could not be sealed. He had to deal with so many people that it was impossible to avoid every risk.

Reaching Dover, he passed through the Customs and Immigration to reach the ramp leading down to the Ostend ferry.

This time he was travelling on a forged passport made out in the name of Peter Meadows, an industrial agent from North London. The officials at the barriers had no particular interest in him and soon he was idling over a late lunch and a bottle of wine.

The grey dunes of the Belgian coast came into sight whilst he was still sitting in the dining room. As he stared out at them over the sea, his thoughts strayed back to the other phone calls from Mr X.

One of them was a long and amorous post-mortem on the time that Rita had spent with the man at his place. He suddenly realised that the man might have stayed at the flat in Newman Street for all he knew, and he decided to bug the next place with a microphone until he realised that it would be impossible to keep it going for a fortnight at a time. He shrugged off plans for as far ahead as that and concentrated on the problems heaped on him by the sudden appearance of this man who had it in his power to wreck his trade and threaten his safety. The dangerous implications of it were clear enough.

'When he comes back next time, do your best to find out everything you can about his real identity – get it?'

The voice increased its brash Yankee intonation. 'We've got him tabbed for the drug racket – we can put the squeeze on him any time for that, but if we can dig up his legit hideout and his real business, we'll have him cold.'

Rita broke in with a string of objections about how tight-lipped Golding was about everything.

'Look, sweetheart, we're sitting on a goldmine, see? You do what you're told – haven't you got any idea where he goes when he leaves you?'

'I once found a luggage office ticket in his pocket for Euston station – so I suppose he goes up North. He gave me a yarn about going to Manchester once, but I didn't believe him.'

'Well, have a good hunt around the flat – he may have left something besides that ticket.'

'I tell you it's hopeless,' retaliated Rita. 'If I start that, he'll soon smell a rat. I don't trust him; he's as hard as hell under the surface.'

The end of the call took on a harder note from the man.

'Look, quit bellyaching! We're on the edge of the sweetest bit of blackmail you could think of. Golding will pay a lot to keep my mouth shut. He must be making a fortune out of that racket. And what if he does take a poke at you – it's worth it, isn't it? As soon as we've got all we want to know, you can tell him to stuff his flat.'

Paul pondered over this until the boat reached Ostend and he was called down to the car deck.

He drove off onto the quay, passed through the barriers where the officials were far more interested in his car than the driver, and then out into the streets of Ostend. He took to the right-hand side of the road without a second thought. His German origins and the frequent trips to the Continent made him equally at home on either side.

He drove out onto the auto-route to Brussels and settled the big grey car down to a steady eighty miles an hour. Now he had time to mull over the last phone call on the tape. Again, there was a big gap in the plot, but it seemed that since the last call, Rita had mentioned the wall safe to her boyfriend. He had sent some crony of his over to Newman Street to crack it open. The man must have been an expert, as Paul had examined the lock minutely without finding any trace of interference.

The taped voices echoed again in Jacobs' mind as the Jaguar hammered slightly on the bad joints in the concrete surface.

'Are you sure there's nothing at all anywhere to give us a lead on where he really has his pad?' demanded the man's voice, sounding like the dialogue from a third-rate gangster film. 'Those five passports in the safe make it a dead cert that he gets all his stuff from the Continent, but there was damn-all to give a lead on his real name over here.'

'I tell you there's nothing more – he's never said a word about it and I've been through his clothes a dozen times –not even a tailor's label on any of them. He knows the score too well to be caught like that.'

She paused and hurried on.

'I hope to God he doesn't catch on yet that I'm in this – I hate to think what he'd do.'

Paul Jacobs smiled grimly as the exit for Ghent flashed by the window. 'You'll never know, sweetheart,' he whispered.

A few miles further on the dull day closed in towards dusk and he switched on his side lights. Odd bits of the obnoxiously carnal phone calls came back to him as he neared the Belgian capital. He thrust them aside and his orderly chess player's mind arranged a summary of the position.

Firstly, some unknown man had cut Rita out from behind his back. That was a nuisance, but not a dangerous one. She suited him very well in a physical sense, but she was replaceable. Women – apart from his wife, who belonged to his other world of sacred respectability – were like the car he was driving. They were beautiful and a novelty when new, but should be changed before they got old. They could be changed as easily as a car – and as often – if one was willing to pay the price. Secondly, this man knew of his narcotic smuggling racket and was preparing to blackmail him over it.

Thirdly, the unknown Mr X did not know his true identity – that he was Paul Jacobs, antique silver dealer of Cardiff. But he was working on it and had to be stopped.

It was dark when he reached the outskirts of Brussels. Driving through the confusing maze of roads with the ease of familiarity, he arrived at the Boulevard Adolphe Maximus and checked in at his hotel.

A porter drove his car around to the garages at the rear, while he went up for a bath and a rest before dinner. He lay on his bed before dressing, staring up at the ornamental plaster of the high ceiling.

He chewed his lip as he polished up the plan that had been born when he helped the giggling Rita from the club the night before.

When the pieces had all fitted into place in his mind, he swung himself off the bed to dress. As soon as dinner was over, he went out into the bright lights of the city. After walking a little way from the hotel, he hailed a taxi. Using good French, with a deliberate German accent just to confuse the trail in the unlikely event of there ever being one, he gave directions to the driver. The car turned into the Boulevard Leopold and ran parallel to its overhead viaduct for some distance. Then they cut across in the direction of the Gare du Nord. Outside the station, Paul paid the man off and walked into the station entrance. As soon as the cab drove off, he turned sharply to his right and walked up the Rue de Brabant.

Some distance up, he turned off into a side street and, after a few more right-angled turns, found a shuttered bakery on the comer of an alleyway. The cracked paint above the front of the shop announced that it was Emil Corot et Fils. He dived into the gloomy tunnel alongside the shop and found a door, almost invisible in the darkness. Paul rapped hard on the peeling panels. Three heavy knocks, a pause – three more knocks, softer this time.

After a long delay, there was the sound of bolts and a chain being unfastened. The door creaked open, but no face appeared. Jacobs stepped inside and walked down a short passage to another door, which led to a dimly lit storeroom, filled with sacks and cardboard cartons. A thick powdering of flour lay over everything.

He turned inside the room and waited to greet an old man who shuffled after him from the passage. They spoke in French, but the bent old baker had little to say. He had red, inflamed eyes and a drooping moustache. Like his storeroom, he was covered in white dust.

He slouched across the room to a pile of cartons marked *Syrian Figs*. Opening the tops of two of them, he took out a layer of cellophane-wrapped cooking figs, each parcel being about half a kilo. Beneath this layer was a layer of thin plastic bags containing white powder. There were several dozen in all and the old man carefully took them out and stacked them on top of a box.

'I've already unpacked them from the figs,' he muttered unnecessarily. Paul was not interested; he knew well enough how the drugs had arrived from the Levant. Each carton contained fifty kilos of figs, a hundred packets in all. In certain marked cartons, the fig packets one layer deep in the box had a plastic bag of heroin or morphine embedded through the fruit.

Old man Corot shuffled in his senile way to a large cupboard against the wall. He took out two smart fawn-coloured suitcases and brought them over to the pile of drugs.

'They were brought here last week,' he grunted, 'Just like you said.'

Paul's organisation had worked smoothly again. The special cases had been made in Antwerp and delivered to Corot pending his arrival.

'You'd better do it, I don't understand these things,' grumbled the baker, standing back.

Paul opened the cases on the floor, threw the lids right back and began fumbling with both the locks and the lid hinges. In a few seconds, the whole of the taffeta lining came out in a single piece, stiffened beneath by a layer of fibreboard. Between the lining and the leather of the case, there was sufficient room to stack the thin plastic envelopes of drugs and still have room to spare.

He stowed his illegal imports away and slid the linings back into place.

'OK, Papa ... ready for another trip.'

He picked up the light and apparently empty cases and made for the door.

Without a word of farewell on either side, Jacobs left the alley and walked back to the Gare du Nord where he caught another taxi back to his hotel.

Next morning he went down to the garage behind the hotel and looked out the foreman mechanic.

'I'm having some trouble with my carburation,' he lied, patting the vast bonnet of the Jaguar. 'Do you think you can get the Jaguar agent to check the carburettors while I'm away? I've to go to Liège for a night, but I can easily go on the train. I want the car perfect for the trip back to England.'

With a few words more and a liberal tip, he had given himself a first class excuse for being away from the hotel without the car for the better part of two days.

Collecting his cases, which he filled with some of his clothes and an assortment of stuff brought over in the car, he went by taxi to the airport.

Here he caught a plane for Paris and Dublin, booked weeks earlier in yet another name.

The amount of forward organising he had to do was immense. He worked out the details of each trip for a couple of months ahead, never using the same method or route more than once a year. It was the regular travellers that attracted the attention of the Customs, especially in the winter season. Every time Paul was in London, or abroad, he spent a great deal of time booking planes, rail tickets, hotels and arranging delivery of drugs. In fact it was like any other import business, but made more difficult by its clandestine nature and the sweat of having to do all the 'office boy' routine himself.

Before he boarded the plane for Dublin, he put on a Germanic-looking raincoat and armed himself with a German newspaper and magazine. He used a passport, forged in Whitechapel, made out for Hans Korb, a textile representative from the Federal German Republic. There was such a boom in German-Irish industrial relations that such visitors were ten-a-penny in Eire and on arrival at Dublin, and the Immigration and Customs gave him the most cursory looking-over. They idly turned over the cloth samples that he had carefully provided himself with before leaving London then made the magic chalk marks on the cases.

He had a meal in a hotel, shed his German coat and identity, and caught a train to Rosslare. The journey via the Fishguard ferry and train to Paddington took him all of the rest of the day and much of the early hours of the following morning.

When the train approached Cardiff, though it was the middle of the night, he retired to the toilet and afterwards kept a wary eye out for anyone who might recognise him. There was no one, and he arrived in London tired, but undetected, with his precious cargo. At the station, he took a taxi to Bloomsbury and got out near the University Union. The streets were deserted and he went as near as possible to his second hideout to reduce the risk of a strolling constable getting suspicious about his cases.

He walked to a block of service flats in Fenton Square and let himself into one on the third floor. This was his other pied-a-terre in London, known only to himself and Snigger. Rita Ronalde had no idea it existed and it was from here that Paul did all his narcotics distribution, with the help of the barman at the Nineties

He pushed the cases wearily under the bed, set the

alarm for 8 a.m., and had a few hours' sleep in the single bedroom. All too soon the clanging of the clock woke him. He washed and shaved, then emptied the clothes from the fake cases into a similar pair of normal ones.

He made his way back to Euston, had some breakfast and caught the Irish Mail to Belfast travelling via Holyhead. From there he crossed the border into Eire and went back to Dublin. As far as the border officials were concerned, he was Arthur Graham, an English textile representative. They had never seen him or his samples before and he aroused no interest.

All the times had been carefully worked out many weeks before, so that he arrived at Dublin airport a mere hour before the take off. He became Hans Korb once again and arrived in the Belgian capital late on the Thursday evening.

Next morning, the garage foreman sorrowfully explained that nothing could be found wrong with the carburettors of the Mark X. Another large tip helped him to get over his grief and, by mid-morning, Paul Jacobs was thundering back over the auto-route towards Ostend, the car seeming none the worse for having its carburettors disembowelled for nothing.

At the Dover end of the trip, he had the most rigorous Customs examination of the whole trip. Whether the officers happened to pick on him as someone on whom to vent their mid-winter boredom or whether they had any reason to suspect him, Paul did not know.

He stood by the car with the complacency of an easy conscience as they spent twenty minutes looking through all his luggage and examining every nook and cranny of the car. An officer in overalls even crawled beneath the car with a torch to see if anything was strapped to the half-shaft housings or steering gear.

They eventually waved him away with that stony stare that only Customs Officers and police constables can generate. By five o'clock on the Friday evening, he was putting the Jaguar away in the garage behind Newman Street.

Rita was expecting him this time and had carefully left off her jeans to please him. To please him even more, she was wearing a negligee and a pair of earrings – nothing else. Within ten minutes, she had taken off the earrings and he had attended to the negligee. He was so occupied for the rest of the evening that he had no opportunity to get to his hidden recorder.

Next morning, Rita went out to look for a new dress in Oxford Street, in preparation for his promised celebration next evening. As soon as she was well clear, he squatted down on the bedroom floor and took out the machine. Sure enough, there was an inch thickness of tape on the spool. The unwelcome voice of the 'cuckoo in the nest' grated on Paul's ears when he played it back. Again, there was nothing to give away the man's identity. Rita infuriated him by using strings of mushily endearing names, but never once his real one. After some archly suggestive byplay, the voices got down to business.

'I still haven't found a thing to show who he really is,' complained the woman.

'You must do … for God's sake, Rita, he must have some steady pad somewhere … look, stop messing about and find out.'

'I tell you I can't,' she stormed angrily. 'You don't know him; he's as tight as a bloody oyster. No papers anywhere, no nothing.'

They carried on in this way for a few minutes, the man complaining and the girl making excuses. Then they calmed down and the last few feet of the tape were more semi-erotic slush.

Paul punched the stop button with vicious finality. He replaced the equipment, but didn't bother to set it ready again. Its job was done, he thought, as he tightened the screws and rearranged the dresses over the floor.

Rita came back about twelve and he took her out to lunch, keeping his mood exactly as usual in spite of the slow burning fury at this silly little fool for putting his whole way of life in danger by her petty love affairs. In the afternoon, she went off to do some work for a photographer, which gave him time to prepare the next phase of his scheme.

As well as this type of work, she had been a club hostess, a stripper, and part of a cabaret act in the ten years since she had come from Trieste as the bride of an English soldier. She had left him after three months in England and had kept herself by means of these various jobs, all of which depended on her face and her figure, as well as her wits.

The photography that she posed for was for the mildly obscene *Cheese Cake* magazine – known to the local police as the 'garters and gum boots' business. It paid well and gave her something to do when her man-friend was away.

After Rita had left, Paul went by Tube to Shepherd's Bush and called at a car hire firm. He picked an inconspicuous grey Ford Anglia and hired it until Monday morning, giving a totally fictitious name and address to the salesman. He drove off along Western Avenue, keeping on until he reached open country beyond Denham. Then he turned off into a series of minor roads for another ten miles until he came to Cuckoo Hill, well out in the countryside.

Jacobs pulled up at the top of the hill and sat looking down the road with approval. He saw the long straight slope with a sudden bend at the bottom where the road turned right across a bridge. Below a low parapet, there was a deep drop into a ravine where a stream flowed beneath the road.

His survey completed, he turned and drove slowly back until he came to a small side road about half a mile from the hill. A few hundred yards along this lane, he came to a rough lay-by, where road menders had dumped heaps of gravel.

Pulling the Ford well off the road, he took out the jack and removed one of the rear wheels. Leaving the car jacked up, he put the wheel in the boot and locked everything up. Now he had a means of getaway all laid on, the missing wheel being a camouflage for any nosey-parker who happened to come by during the Sunday.

He walked away in the opposite direction to a village a mile away that he had seen on the map. Here he caught a Green Line bus back to London and his flat.

The stage was set for the following night's drama.

Chapter Three

'I'm sorry, Mr Laskey, but as her husband you are the next-of-kin; the responsibility is all yours.'

Mr Smythe, the Oldfield coroner, looked over his steel-rimmed spectacles at the indignant husband of the late Rita Ronalde. Her real name had been Laskey, after the soldier who had brought her from Italy.

'But I haven't seen her for nine years. Why should I have to pay for burying her now?'

Laskey stood aggressively before the coroner. He was a short, ugly man in a shabby suit.

Mr Smythe sighed and shuffled his papers.

'I'm sorry, but there it is. Either she's your wife, or she isn't ... if she left any money, you might get something that will more than cover the funeral expenses.'

Laskey's eyes opened a little wider.

'She wouldn't leave a bent ha'penny to me,' he said suspiciously.

'If she hasn't left a will, you'll be entitled,' countered the shrewd country solicitor, knowing that that would strike a sympathetic chord in the scruffy man before him.

Laskey sat down thoughtfully and waited for the coroner to finish scrabbling through his papers.

This was the day following the discovery of the wreckage of the Sunbeam. Mr Smythe was holding a preliminary opening of the inquest at the local police station. The County Constabulary wanted the usual week or ten days to make inquiries, so to dispose of the body in the meantime, the coroner had to take evidence of identity from a near relative before giving the order to allow burial.

Oldfield was a small town about five miles from Cuckoo Hill, which came within Smythe's jurisdiction, much to his annoyance on this particular day. He leaned over the table in the Inspector's Room to speak to the police sergeant who was waiting attendance on him.

'If you'll hand me that disposal order, I'll sign it now and Mr Laskey can take it to the Registrar before he closes.'

The sergeant, a tall man with a magnificent moustache passed a yellow form across to the coroner.

'It is burial, not cremation, eh?' asked Mr Smythe, with another penetrating stare over his glasses.

The bereaved, but unmoved, husband nodded emphatically. It costs more to burn 'em, he thought, and for all I know the bitch hasn't left a penny towards it.

He left in a few moments clutching his slip of paper. As soon as the door of the office closed behind him, Sergeant Burrell got up.

'Not having a post-mortem, sir?' His tone was one of guarded rebuke.

Smythe shook his ancient head.

'Pointless, quite pointless, Burrell. Your grandmother could tell us the cause of death after a crash like that. We don't need to drag a pathologist over here just to tell us what we know already.'

Burrell suspected that he was thinking of the few guineas he would save on the pathologist's fee, but he kept quiet. No point in arguing with the old codger, he thought. Even in this rural neck of the woods, the ancient power of the coroner was still absolute and Smythe was as pig-headed as they come.

The little solicitor-cum-coroner jammed on his bowler and made for the door.

'Must rush, Burrell, got a client coming at twelve. I've adjourned until Friday week.'

The sergeant nodded.

'Yes, sir. We should have all the statements by then – not that there's likely to be many. The inspector's handling it, but I know he's got next to nothing to go on. No eyewitnesses – can't find the chap she was living with. Only the farmhand who found the wreck and the husband will be able to give any evidence worth hearing.'

Smythe nodded his head like a marionette.

'Too bad, these London people coming out here to get drunk and litter the place with their bodies and their cars! We'll just have to call it accidental death and leave it at that ... look, I must go.'

He looked hurriedly at his watch, grabbed his battered briefcase and scurried out, headed for the more lucrative trade of conveyancing Oldfield's real property.

Some time later, the station inspector bustled in and joined his sergeant over a cup of strong police tea.

'Sorry I couldn't get back, Burrell. Everything go all right?'

The sergeant described the short inquest for him.

'That husband seemed a fly sort of bird. Where did they dig him up from?'

'The Met found him in Luton. They went to the address we found on the woman's driving licence, a place in the West End. Nobody there, apparently, but they found a cleaner who used to have the occasional nip of gin with this Ronalde woman. She said her name was really Laskey and that she was separated from her husband who lived in Luton. So the Bedfordshire police soon unearthed him, with an uncommon name like that.'

The sergeant studied the tea leaves in his clip as if seeking inspiration there.

'Funny set-up,' he said at last. 'Are the Met boys going to find this chap she was living with, I wonder?'

The inspector looked dubious.

'They don't sound very hopeful, and quite frankly, I

don't think they're going to strain their gut very hard to look. They say they've got better things to do than look for a coroner's witness, not that he'd be any good if we found him; he wasn't there when the crash occurred.'

'He's taken a powder, has he?'

'Looks like it; not a sign of him. No man's stuff in the flat – yet the cleaner woman says that this chap had a couple of suits in the wardrobe last week. He's obviously some sugar daddy who wants to keep his nose clean. He's not likely to come forward and get his name in the paper for his wife to read, is he?'

The inspector poured another cup of tea from the chipped brown pot.

'Old Smythe has adjourned for ten days, then?'

'Yes, that should be plenty of time for us. Unless the radio appeal brings in anything, we've got damn-all to do except check on the car.'

'Where is it now?'

Burrell jerked a thumb over his shoulder.

'In the station yard. We got it in last night. You saw it before it was moved, didn't you?'

'Yes, a hell of a mess … must have been a twenty-foot drop from that bridge to the stream. I suppose we'd better get the chap of the Traffic Division to have a look at the wreckage. It'll be one more witness, to swell the band for appearances sake!'

Sergeant Burrell nodded unenthusiastically.

'Suppose so, though with the smell of booze that was hanging around, I don't think the state of the brakes and steering are going to make much odds. Still, I'll get that chap Johnson over to look at it. Better not get as slap-dash as old Smythe.'

The inspector looked up. 'What d'you mean?'

'He isn't going to have a post-mortem on the woman, says it's a waste of time – he really means a waste of money. Anybody would think he had to pay the pathologist out of his own pocket!'

The inspector made wet circles on the tray with the bottom of his cup.

'It would be nice to find a broken track rod or something like that – though with an almost new Sunbeam like that, it's hardly likely. I suppose she was coming down the hill like the clappers and ran out of road at the bottom.'

Burrell grunted.

'She stank of brandy. There was a half-empty bottle on the floor. About the only thing that didn't get broken.'

He went out to the charge room to ring up the Traffic Division in headquarters, cursing Londoners who used Oldfield as a graveyard for their cars and corpses.

Conrad Draper stood glowering down at Berwick Street from a third-floor window. An unlit cigar hung loosely from his fleshy lips as he stared down at the crowds of Soho. The floors below belonged to a film company, but this upper storey was given over to the Draper betting shop empire. From behind the door of his ornate office, there came the ceaseless clatter of typewriters and jangle of telephones as his staff worked away at taking money from the 'mugs'.

His mind was a long way from horse racing at the moment. He had been out of town at a race meeting on the previous day and had only heard about Rita's death that morning. There was nothing in the newspapers; road deaths were no longer news unless more than four people lost their lives at once, but he had got the information from the Soho grapevine within ten minutes of setting foot back in London.

His informant had been 'Irish' O'Keefe, who was Draper's bodyguard and yes man. It was Irish who had got him the hot tip about Golding's racket and the same man had been waiting that morning to tell him of the death of his latest girlfriend.

After a ten-minute rage, untinged by any sorrow, Conrad had sent Irish out again to scour the district for any more information, especially as to the present whereabouts of Paul Golding. Now Conrad was fuming with impatience, waiting for O'Keefe to come back. He chewed on the end of his cigar as he looked up and down Berwick Street trying to get a glimpse of Irish returning. He detested cigars and could never bear to actually light one, but a cigar was part of the American gangster image that was his idol. Whenever he thought of it, he jammed one between his teeth and suffered it until the desire for a cigarette overcame him.

He could still see no sign of the little Irishman outside and, with a snort of anger, Conrad flung himself down in the great swivel chair behind his mahogany desk.

The top was covered with an array of phones, a Dictaphone and intercoms in the best American tradition. He selected a button and jabbed it viciously with a finger the size of a small banana.

A tinny voice came through a speaker on the desk.

'Yes, Mr Draper?'

'Where the hell is Irish?' he barked. 'Has he been in since lunch?'

'No, Mr Draper, not since he left you this morning.'

Even through the intercom, the girl's voice sounded scared. This was what Draper wanted: a big man's staff should be frightened of him. He flicked the switch off without replying and stalked back to the window.

Suddenly noticing the big cheroot stuck in his mouth, he tore it out angrily and flung it onto the window ledge. He felt in the pockets of his drape suit for a packet of cigarettes and lit up with shaking hands. Inhaling deeply, he went back to his survey of the pavements below.

Though the office was big, he seemed too large for it. His wrestler's shoulders and big head with its carefully waved hair seemed to fill the window as he glowered down looking for his stooge.

It would be wrong to say that he was grieving after Rita Ronalde – like Paul Jacobs, his philosophy was that 'skirts' were disposable and easily replaceable. But he was intensely annoyed at the injury to his own pride.

That such a promising bit of stuff should have been snatched from his grasp after only a few weeks' enjoyment was a personal affront. And Conrad Draper, King of the Betting Shops, did not tolerate personal affronts.

He was sure that Rita's death was no accident Though he had only the barest details from Irish, the fact that Golding had vanished, coupled with the fact that he had been ready to spring his blackmail scheme within a matter of days, spelt only one thing to his mind, soaked as it was in the lore of Al Capone: she must have been 'rubbed out'.

He turned to the empty room and waved his cigarette as if he was addressing a board meeting.

'If she was busted up in that car on her own account, well fair enough,' he said aloud. 'Serve the silly bitch right if she can't hold her liquor. But if that bastard Golding has found out about me and croaked her for it – well, he's got me, Conrad Draper, to reckon with.'

He actually tapped himself on the chest as he spoke the last words. As he did so, the door opened, and Irish slipped in. He never walked into a room normally. He always sidled in through a six-inch gap.

O'Keefe caught his boss in the act of tapping himself in the middle of his gaudy brocade waistcoat.

'Bad chest, boss?'

Conrad hurriedly put his hand down and glared at his sidekick.

'Where the hell have you been … south of France?'

Irish looked hurt. He was small, skinny, and incredibly ugly.

'Haven't I just been doing what you asked me,' he

whined in the accents of the Dublin back streets. 'I've been bashing me feet all day round the manor and damn all to show for it.'

The big bookie glowered down at him.

'You must have got something – you can't be as bloody dim as you look.'

Irish shrugged. Draper's abuse was like water off a duck's back to him.

'The Golding feller has taken a powder all right. I've been talking with Minnie, the cleaner. She let me in with her pass key. The dicks have been there already, but only routine. They ain't had no buzz about it being a killing.'

'What d'you find?'

'Sweet Fanny Adams. Some of her clothes there, but none of the gent's. Minnie says that a couple of her pussies had gone – one of 'em a mink.'

Conrad paced back to the window and stared out.

'Anybody know when she left the place?'

'Minnie was there Saturday morning – she was there then – so was Golding.'

'Find anything else there – papers or anything?'

'Nope. I'm telling you, boss, he must have been through that place with a bleeding microscope before he scarpered.'

'Minnie know anything about him?'

'No, and she don't miss much. Cost me a fiver to get in too, she's a sharp old crone, is Minnie,' he added hopefully, chinking some coins in his pocket.

Conrad ignored the hint.

'What about the rozzers –they been poking about?'

Irish nodded.

'Only a PC from the nick – no tecs. Something about the inquest, Minnie said. She told 'em where to find Rita's old man – up Luton way.'

Conrad turned his back on O'Keefe for a moment and the little man covertly pocketed a couple of cigars from the box on the desk. He just made it in time, as Draper swung round and ground his cigarette butt into the floor with a heel.

Conrad slumped back in his chair.

'This Minnie, she doesn't know any other place that Golding might hole up in, does she?'

'Nope. As far as I was after making out, he's a real will-o'-the-wisp. Just vanished the minute he put his foot outside the dame's flat.'

'She must know something,' snapped Conrad angrily digging the point of a paper knife into his desk.

'He came and went like the bleeding wind itself,' said Irish firmly. 'Minnie said that Rita complained to her once that Golding didn't trust her – wouldn't tell her anything about his affairs.'

This squared with what Conrad had heard from Rita and he accepted it with an angry snort.

'What d'you think, Irish, you reckon he done for her?'

Without waiting for an answer, he plunged on.

'Why's he shoved off so fast? He couldn't have known she was dead by the Monday morning; there was nothing in the papers. Damn, he must have croaked her, the bastard!'

Irish turned his hands palms up, expressively.

'Search me, guv'nor. He's been over the flat rubbing off his dabs from the door handles. I looked 'specially for that. I know when a joint's been gone over, having bin in the trade, like.'

Draper looked up at him sharply.

'Are you sure?'

Irish nodded emphatically.

'Sure I'm sure. Not that it proves that he knocked her off. If he was in the dope racket, he wouldn't leave his dabs about, killing or no killing.'

Conrad threw the knife down violently and stalked back to the window.

'I don't know. It stinks to me. I reckon he got wind of her being shacked up with me and fixed her.'

'But she had a car crash – aren't the rozzers as quiet as the little lambs themselves?'

'Pah! Those country coppers wouldn't notice it if the back of her head was blown off ... they've all got pure minds out there. If Golding wanted to fix her, he'd do it all right. He's another smart Alec, but he won't get the drop on me!' He finished with a roar and did a bit more chest tapping.

Irish looked puzzled.

'What's all the beef about? She was only a dame; he wasn't getting at you.'

Conrad swung around from the window, his great body in a half crouch, hands open and elbows crooked, as if he was coming out of his corner in the ring.

'Look, I pay you to snoop into other people's business, not mine!' he snarled. 'Now shurrup and beat it!'

O'Keefe, quite unabashed, coughed and jingled his loose coins again.

'I had some expense, what with Minnie and that.'

Draper unwound and dipped into his breast pocket. He unrolled a note from a thick wad of fivers and flung it at Irish.

'Now grease off – and keep your ears to the ground.'

His private eye oiled out through a crack in the door and left the self-appointed king of the bookies to himself. Conrad lit another cigarette with fingers that had become even more unsteady. After a few puffs, he ground it out in an ashtray.

'If Golding killed my bint, I'll fix him – he can't do this to me.'

A tremor that was only partly rage shook him and he clutched the comer of the desk.

'I'll have a fix – just for my nerves,' he muttered. 'This is a special occasion.'

He crossed the room and slipped the catch down on the lock. Going back to his desk, he unlocked a drawer and took out a small chromium tin, from which he took a spirit lamp, syringe, and tea spoon. From another part of the drawer he took out a flat tin and removed the lid to expose a collection of little polythene bags, the size of a railway ticket. He tore the top off one, tipped the few grains of white powder from it into the spoon, and added some water from a carafe on the desk. He lit the lamp with his lighter and boiled the few drops of fluid. While it was cooling on the ink stand, he took off his coat and rolled up his shirtsleeve.

Handling the syringe clumsily in his shaking fingers, he sucked up the fluid in the spoon and jabbed the needle into a fold of skin which he pinched up on his arm. As Conrad pushed home the glass plunger, a swelling appeared indistinctly in the flesh which he rubbed away impatiently after pulling the needle out.

Draper put all his apparatus away and slumped down in his chair to wait for the heroin to take effect. He was a newcomer to the drug and was still taking infrequent jabs into the skin, not into a vein like the more advanced addicts. The effects from a skin-pop were slower than the mainliners and it was ten minutes before he felt the welcome calmness spreading through his system like a wave of comforting warmth.

He lit another cigarette and inhaled deeply. Leaning back in the chair, he addressed a nude mural on the opposite wall.

'I'll find you, Paul bloody Golding. I'm going to screw a few thousand out of you and then take over your racket.' His face hardened, even through the euphoric haze of heroin.

'But if I find out that you croaked my bird, sonny, I'll kill you!'

Chapter Four

A stubble-haired man in blue dungarees came into the charge room of Oldfield police station. He was carrying a short piece of twig and had a worried look on his round face.

'Sarge, is the inspector in his office?'

Burrell looked up from his Occurrences book and nodded.

'What's up? A sawn-through steering column?'

His facetiousness was lost on the vehicle examiner, a constable in the Traffic Division. Part of Johnson's job was to report on the road worthiness of vehicles involved in accidents or on charges of negligent maintenance.

He held up the dirty bit of stick.

'Look at this ... from that Alpine outside.'

Burrell brushed up his moustache and peered at the thing. It was a fairly straight twig about a foot long.

'What's so wonderful about it?'

The mechanic turned the twig in his fingers.

'It .was jammed under the throttle control rod. How the hell did it get there?'

The sergeant looked at him with new interest.

'Was the throttle stuck open?'

Johnson shook his head.

'No, but it might have been before the crash. The stick looks as if it was broken off.'

Burrell came around the desk.

'Let's ask the guv'nor.'

He tapped the inspector's door and a moment later the three men were huddled over the stick in the inner office.

'See, there's grease on this end,' Johnson pointed to stains on the bar. 'But the other end has snapped.'

'Could it have got there at the time of the crash?' hazarded Burrell.

'How ... there was no hedge there? The car came down the road, through a wire fence and over the grass bank – no bushes anywhere near. This is a hazel branch.'

They adjourned to the station yard and leant over the twisted remains of the red Sunbeam. The engine had been pushed back in the frame by the impact, but the twin carburettors were undamaged.

'The stick was jammed under here,' explained Johnson, indicating the gap between the butterfly control arm and the venturi tube of the rear carburettor.

Burrell studied the front of the scuttle which separated the engine compartment from the inside of the car.

'Look, see those scratches ... they could have been caused by the other end of the stick.'

On the flat partition, which was undamaged, there were several wavering lines gouged in the coating of black grease. These were at the same level as the butterfly control.

Johnson nodded excitedly.

'If the stick was longer, it would reach from there to the carburettor.'

The inspector, a lifelong sceptic, straightened his back.

'But it isn't, is it?' he said.

Burrell took the stick from Johnson and looked at the broken end again. 'If we could find the other bit that matched this ... and if it was the right length ... and if it had grease on the end ...' His voice trailed off.

The inspector moved. 'Come on, my car's over there,' he said.

Within five minutes of starting to search the bank of the culvert on Cuckoo Hill, Johnson had found the missing twig. It was directly under the parapet, in the centre of the skid marks. It was half as long as the first piece, it had black grease on one end and the other end had broken in such a way as to make it clear to the most obstinate juror that it had once been continuous with the bigger twig.

'This is it,' enthused Johnson. 'Some bloody jiggery-pokery here all right.'

The inspector took it more soberly.

'You mean our troubles are just beginning. I'm already wishing I'd never heard of you, Johnson.'

The practical sergeant was studying the two bits, which he held end-to-end. 'If it's the right length, that will add a bit more weight to our argument.'

They drove back to Oldfield and visited the local Rootes agent. The mystified owner led them to a new Alpine in his showroom and watched them while they vanished under the bonnet. To Johnson's delight, the total length of the two twigs exactly fitted the distance between the scuttle and the throttle control.

They went back to the police station and held a council of war.

'I'm going to speak to Headquarters about this,' decided the inspector. 'This is going to be a London job, through and through. If our chaps have got any sense, they'll give it to the Yard straight away. No point in the County arsing about with it; all the background is going to be up in Town.'

Johnson looked as if his pension prospects had been snatched away from him, but the inspector's forecast was quite right. Before lunch, the Divisional Detective Chief Inspector had been down to verify the facts and after speaking to the chief constable on the phone, had rung the Central Office of the Metropolitan Police to ask for assistance.

At four thirty, the Yard men arrived, a chief inspector and a detective sergeant.

The senior man was the well-known Archie Benbow, known to the Met as Admiral Benbow. He was a thickset man with bulbous features, bearing a startling resemblance to Mr Khrushchev.

His assistant, Alan Bray, was a very young sergeant, recently made up from detective constable. He was bursting with enthusiasm and his appearance generally reminded the cynical Sergeant Burrell of a keen country curate.

The two newcomers went over the car again and studied the pieces of stick, which Johnson was guarding as if they were the Holy Grail. They adjourned into the inspector's office and sat around the table.

Benbow removed his Moscow-type fedora and folded his hands on the stained wood before him. He was well aware of the stock joke about his resemblance to the Soviet ex-leader and did all he could to perpetuate the gimmick. His belted raincoats and large hats were all part of the act, but this harmless farce took nothing away from his ability as a first class detective.

He started the ball rolling. 'Now then ... what's been done so far?'

The Oldfield inspector went on the defensive at once.

'Well, very little so far; we didn't know there was anything fishy about it until this morning.'

Benbow puffed out his podgy cheeks. 'OK ... now, do we all agree that the bit of stick jammed under the throttle means a deliberate attempt to crash the car?'

He glared around as if defying anyone to deny it.

'So who could have done it?'

No one spoke and he went on. 'Couldn't be the deceased ... if she wanted to knock herself off, she'd go it a darned sight easier by keeping her foot on the pedal. So that means someone else did it for her – and that means murder!'

This was the first time that day that the word had

actually been used and there was a thoughtful silence. Everyone had been skirting around it for the past few hours, but now the Admiral's blunt words had broken the ice and there was confused murmuring of suggestions and comments.

Benbow held up his head in best United Nations manner. 'All right, all right, let's get the facts straight.'

IIis sergeant, the angelic-looking Bray, cut in with an objection, voiced with a nervous determination.

'But no one would risk murder this way – she might not have been killed – we've all seen far worse crashes than this where the driver has got up and walked away.'

Benbow gave him a sorrowful look.

'And how do you know the crash killed her? She might have been shot, stabbed, strangled, poisoned ...' He left the sentence in mid-air.

'The post-mortem ...' Bray's voice trailed off weakly. Benbow looked at the inspector and then at the local sergeant. They both shook their heads slowly and sadly the Admiral slapped his hands on the table sharply.

'See, Bray, keep your trap shut then you can't put your foot in it.' He smiled suddenly and disarmingly at his sergeant, taking all the sting out of his words. 'Well, we can soon fix a post-mortem, can't we?'

Benbow looked brightly at the local policemen and their sheepish faces made his jaw drop.

'Oh God ... no ... not that!'

The Oldfield inspector nodded sheepishly.

'Buried the day before yesterday,' he admitted. 'Sorry, but our local coroner's not too keen on holding post-mortems, especially on what he calls obvious road accidents.'

Archie Benbow sighed. 'Still, it could have been worse,' he said. 'She could have been cremated.' He stiffened suddenly. 'Christ, she wasn't was she?'

'No, she was buried ... here in the local cemetery.'

The Admiral relaxed.

'Well, we can fix that. As far as I remember, the coroner has power to order an exhumation on one of his own cases, hasn't he?'

Bray shook his head sadly at Benbow.

'No, sir, sorry. If he's held an inquest – even opened one as in this instance – only the Home Secretary can give permission.'

Archie Benbow scowled at his erudite assistant.

'Proper bloody genius, aren't you? Do you read a chapter from Jarvis's text book every night before you go to sleep?'

Bray grinned good-humouredly. 'Do you want me to get it organised, sir?'

Benbow grunted his assent. 'And get hold of one of the forensic chaps from Town to come out and do a post-mortem.'

I think Eustace Soames usually does this part of the Home Counties. And tell the Yard Laboratory to join the party as well.'

Bray went out with Burrell to the charge room to use the telephone while his boss got on with the talking. Archie tapped the pathetically thin folder which contained the few documents so far collected about the Laskey case.

'All we've got here is the fact that this woman lived in an expensive flat in the West End and was kept by some man, so far quite unknown to us.'

The Oldfield inspector nodded. 'That's all we could ruddy-well find out. I'm afraid, apart from the fact that she was separated from her husband, who lives in Luton. Can't see him as a suspect; he didn't want to know about her when we had him here for the inquest.'

Benbow looked thoughtful. 'Better get hold of him again I think, and give him a working over; he may know something that he didn't think he knew at first.'

'He was a full-blown nobody,' commented the

inspector. Said he hadn't seen her for nine years and wasn't madly keen to see her for another nine ... he moaned like hell when old Smythe swung the cost of the funeral on him.'

'Well, he won't have to pay for the exhumation, if that's any comfort to him,' grinned Benbow. 'If Bray does his stuff out there, we should have her up by first light in the morning.

Chapter Five

'It's nice to have you at home at the weekend, Paul.'

The Jacobs family were at home, enjoying tea at the fireside of their Cardiff home. A wicked east wind howled outside and the shaking trees in the garden added to the comfort of being inside.

'Old Ben can look after the shop till Monday,' he drawled in reply. 'We never do much on a Friday afternoon.'

Paul's legitimate business was in a lock-up shop near the docks, where an aged, but experienced, assistant ran the sales during Paul's frequent trips to London to 'buy stock.'

He leant back comfortably against the arm of the settee and looked across at his wife.

She was a calm woman of his own age, by no means glamorous but with considerable character. He had met her in London six years before, when he ran a similar business in Finsbury as a cover for the same smuggling racket. She was a schoolteacher and, by some magic of compatibility, he soon found that he wanted to marry her.

He had a mistress at that time, but his knack of running a double life was already well developed and he found this no bar to a rapid courtship.

His wife wanted to go back to her home in Wales and, as this suited his Jekyll and Hyde existence very well, he sold up and started a shop in Cardiff. At first heavily subsidised from his smuggling, he found to his surprise that after a year or two it began to break even and now was actually paying its way.

His wife had no idea of his other life or of his true identity. She was not over-inquisitive, one of the factors that attracted him to her. She realised that he was of foreign origin, but his carefully prepared story of being an Austrian who had fled the country in 1938 and spent the war in the British Merchant Navy satisfied her completely.

He stretched his feet to the fire and prodded the dog with a toe.

'Better off here than Glasgow, this time last week,' he lied easily.

His wife looked up, her grey eyes looking steadily from a long face free of any make-up.

'Why Glasgow all of a sudden? I thought you did all your buying in London.'

Paul nodded lazily.

'Until now ... a new firm has opened up there, a few points lower in price, so it's worth my while going up to get the edge on the London values.'

He was building up a cover for the future. Now that his usual routine was threatened by the unknown man on the tape, he might need more time away. It was better to prepare the ground beforehand than to make lame excuses later.

The domestic bliss went on undisturbed. With his knack of being able to produce a voluntary schizophrenia, Paul was able to shut his mind at will to the sordid other half of his life. When he was in Cardiff, he really was a respectable antique dealer with a nice respectable house in a select district, a cultured and utterly respectable wife, and a few respectable friends in the local golf club.

The only contact that Jacobs allowed between his two lives were the dates of his next visits to London and the judicious transfusion of his local bank account with illegal money.

Since coming back to Cardiff on the Tuesday, he had spent every day at the shop. He had not bothered to look in his newspaper, rightly presuming that no national daily would bother to report a solitary fatal road accident.

He was confident that no suspicion of foul play would arise and that he could safely reappear in the West End without feeling the heavy hand of the law to fall on his shoulder.

The tremendous crunch he had heard when the speeding Sunbeam had hit the parapet of the bridge on Cuckoo Hill told him that it must certainly be a complete wreck, and that Rita's body had shared in the destruction.

He had rather hoped that the car would have caught fire, but even so, he expected that the injuries to the body would be so severe as to completely confuse the issue, if it was ever raised. Perhaps he would have been less complacent at his fireside if he had known that the police were at that very moment arranging with the Home Office for the exhumation of his late mistress.

Conrad Draper sat at his tycoon-size desk and scanned through the lists of accounts from his betting shops. Saturday morning was a time of reckoning, when he could assess his takings for the week. This was when he kicked out his branch managers who were falling by the wayside and when the 'black spot' was put on clients who were winning too much or too often. Occasionally, he used Saturday morning to pick out the customers who needed his strong-arm boys to call on them to encourage them to hurry up with their debts.

The importance of this routine had driven even the matter of Paul Golding from his head for an hour or two. All the week, Draper had harried Irish O'Keefe for more information on the mysterious drug merchant of Newman Street, but so far, he had turned nothing up of any use.

Plenty of people, especially around Gerrard Street, knew Golding by sight, but very few had any idea that he was a drug runner. No one knew where he went when he left Soho, in spite of all Irish's efforts to wheedle information from the junkies and pushers of the district.

They did no direct business with Golding; he was strictly a wholesaler and never risked the dangers of dealing with a host of small-time traders, who were notorious for their unreliability.

It was on this Saturday morning, when the boss was absorbed in his gambling statistics, that Irish had his first break. O'Keefe tapped on the door of the inner sanctum and slid in like a wraith. He was standing in front of the desk before Conrad realised that he was there. The pouch-eyed bookie jerked his head up in surprise.

'Don't you ever bloody-well knock, Irish,' he rasped. 'What d'you want?'

The little man's mouth cracked open into a grin, exposing a ragged line of yellow teeth.

'I did it, boss, I got a bloke outside. I think he knows something about Golding.'

Draper slammed his accounts folder shut and stood up quickly.

'Does he know who he is? Show him in – fast.'

Irish shook his head sorrowfully.

'He don't know who he is, nor where he goes, but he may know something that might tell you that you're in a bit of a spot.'

Conrad reddened. His coarsely handsome face, thickened by fighting and whisky, scowled down at his sidekick.

'Cut the innuendo, Irish.' He was proud of this word, gleaned from an old movie the week before.

O'Keefe sidetracked into his favourite topic: money.

'It'll cost a few nicker to get him squealing. I had to slip him a fiver to get him as far as this.'

Draper slammed the desk and made the telephones tinkle.

'All right, all right, you flaming Dublin crook, you'll

get it back. Now wheel him in before I flatten your earholes.'

Irish slithered through the door and reappeared with a skinny young man in a bright blue suit. He had long sideburns and a weak receding chin.

'This is Alfie Day,' announced Irish proudly, as if he was presenting a child prodigy. 'He keeps that radio shop in Piper's Court.'

Conrad scowled at the seedy electrician without enthusiasm.

'What d'you lug him up here for?'

Alfie looked uneasily from one to the other.

'I heard that Irish was asking around about Golding … I wondered if a bit of info was worth any bunce to you. I was told to keep my trap shut, mind. I might get the sticky end if he finds out.'

'Depends on what you got to tell me,' grunted Draper.

The radio dealer smiled weakly. 'I thought it might be worth a pony,' he said hopefully. His voice trailed off as he saw the expression on Draper's face.

'Twenty-five! Go and get stuffed, mate. Say your piece and I'll see if I can squeeze you out a fiver.'

'I don't exactly know anything about him – personally – but I did a job for him … he said I was to keep quiet about it.'

Conrad's expression spurred him to carry on quickly.

'He came to me a few months back and asked me to fit a tape recorder to the telephone in this dame's flat – the one that copped it last weekend. It was a cagey job – I had to do it all inside a couple of hours when she was out of the place. He gave me a key and said he'd keep her out of the way long enough for me to fix it up.'

Conrad felt a cold lump grow in the pit of his stomach. 'What then?' he said hollowly.

'I had to make a false bottom in a cupboard for it, and connect the recorder to the telephone junction box in the bedroom.'

Draper's icy patch spread across his middle. He wasn't sure what all this meant, but he felt that it wasn't good for his health. 'Go on!' he said between his teeth.

'Not much more to it,' answered Alfie. 'The motor was wired so that it started to run as soon as the receiver was lifted on the phone. It was transistorised, so it didn't need to warm up – it was ready to go straight away – wouldn't miss a word.'

The betting shop magnate thought for a moment.

'Was this a two-way gadget – could it pick up both callers' voices?'

Alfie nodded. 'Oh, yes … there was an extra big spool fitted so that it would run for over an hour if needed. Golding said that he might have to leave it a couple of weeks at a time.' He looked hopefully at Conrad. 'That's all.'

The big man ignored his hint for a reward.

'How did Golding get on to you? Did he know you before?'

'No, Ray Silver in the Nineties Club recommended me – I'd just done some work on the microphones there.'

'And you don't know anything about this Golding? Did he say where he was from or anything else at all about himself?'

The man in the awful suit shook his head vigorously.

'Nah, he was as tight as a bleeding oyster. Didn't say a dicky bird. He told me what to do, gave me the lolly afterwards and told me to screw my mouth down … I'm taking a risk grassing to you, mister, straight I am.' He ended on a whine.

Conrad stood up, peeled a couple of blue notes off his roll, and gave them to the electrician.

'Right, shove off. You needn't worry about Golding; it's me you want to think about. If you drop a whisper of this to anybody, I'll have your shop turned into a junkyard, right?'

Alfie understood only too well and vanished in record time with his ten pounds clutched in his fist.

When he had gone, Conrad seemed in a better humour.

'Irish, we're going to pay a call on Ray Silver tonight. That slanty-eyed swine has been in with Golding and I didn't know it.'

Chapter Six

Though the rain had stopped late on the Friday night, Oldfield cemetery was little better than a quagmire in the early hours of the next morning.

At six o'clock, it was still pitch dark when a plain blue van drove up to the ornate gates set in the stone wall. A man – a council gravedigger – got out and unlocked the gates in the beam of the van's headlights.

The vehicle passed through and made its way along narrow tarmac roads until it reached the newest graves in one corner. Nearby was a wooden hut. Two more men got down and fetched spades, poles, and canvas from it before trudging through the squelching turf to the most recent burial plot.

Working with their gumboots already plastered in red earth, they erected a screen from the hessian and posts, before starting to remove the fresh soil from the grave. They laboured by the light of two paraffin lamps hung on the poles. The harsh shadows and silhouettes made an eerie pattern as the two undertaker's men watched them from the cab of the van.

The top layers were hard going but, by the time the first flush of grey light appeared in the sky, they had got down to the drier soil and the going was easier.

After this, there was only room for one man at a time in the hole and they took it in turns. The two undertakers ambled over to watch the last stages, and by seven o'clock they saw the spade thumping on the top of the coffin.

A few moments later, the diggers were able to rub the mud from the brass plate and confirm that the box held the last remains of Rita Laskey.

They came up for a quick smoke, then went back to clear the soil from the sides sufficiently to pass two ropes around the coffin. The ends were brought up to the graveside and after a few experimental pulls to make sure that enough earth had been taken out, the workers relaxed.

At exactly seven thirty, the yellow beam of headlights swept through the gates and a black Wolseley drew up behind the van. Sergeant Burrell and a thin man in a raincoat came over to the little group.

The gravediggers touched their caps to the man in plain clothes.

'Morning, Mr Phelps, we've got 'er ready.'

Their boss, the council surveyor, had come to identify the grave to the police sergeant. He took a rolled plan from his coat and studied it by the light of a pressure lamp.

'Laskey ... number nine-two-six. That's the eighteenth in the second row beyond the north roadway.'

He walked down the path with a torch wavering in his hand, counting the headstones and the pathetic heaps of earth.

'That's it, sergeant – that's nine-two-six all right.'

Burrell grunted. He was no great one for getting up in the morning and to be dragged out at six o'clock to take the borough surveyor to a sodden cemetery was no great stimulus to his conversation.

'Get her up, then,' he said shortly to the workman.

They and the two undertakers tailed onto the ropes and with some grunting and squelching, the coffin came free from the grave's muddy bottom. They hauled it up level with the surface and swung its end onto a plank which had been laid across the head of the pit. One of the men slid another plank under the other end and, with the weight taken, they removed the ropes and stood back.

'Better check the plate yourself, sarge,' suggested one of the diggers. He leant over and rubbed the metal with a rag.

Burrell held his torch close and peered at the brass oblong. 'Rita Maria Laskey ... At rest ... eighteenth of November, nineteen-sixty-four,' he read aloud. 'OK lads, take it away – up to the hospital.'

After cleaning as much of the mud off as they could, they carried the box to the van and took it to the mortuary of Oldfield Hospital.

Sergeant Burrell took the surveyor home and then went back to the station to wait for the Yard men and the pathologist. They arrived at eight o'clock, together with a liaison officer from the Yard Forensic Laboratory and, by half past eight, Dr Eustace Soames was starting his examination.

The little mortuary of the district hospital was packed out with the detectives, doctor, mortuary assistant, and the police photographers who lurked in the background with their apparatus.

Again the coffin plaque was checked for continuity of evidence. Then the lid was unscrewed.

Benbow, from experience of previous exhumations, stepped back as the seal was broken, but in this case there was no semi-explosive escape of foul gas. The body had only been down a couple of days and the weather was cold.

The body was photographed before being disturbed, then Burrell, who had seen it before burial, formally identified it to the pathologist. Soames, in rubber boots, long gown, and rubber apron, waited impatiently while the shroud was removed and the body placed on the porcelain slab.

'Come on, come on, I'm playing golf at twelve,' he fretted.

The tubby mortuary attendant, on double time for a Saturday morning and with the prospect of a good tip as well, fussed about arranging instruments.

When Soames was ready to start, the police arranged themselves as close to the white-tiled walls as possible, to be out of range of the splashes for which Soames was notorious.

The bare remains of the girl from Newman Street lay on the dish-shaped slab. The pathologist stood with his gloved hands on his hips, staring intently at every part of it.

There was a pregnant silence.

'Don't expect any miracles from me, Benbow,' he warned. 'She's been washed, her clothes have gone, and she's been dead for nearly a week. The undertakers have pulled her about, buried her, and now dug her up! So I hope you'll appreciate that I'm starting at a disadvantage.'

Benbow looked at the battered corpse lying so still on the white table. He kept telling himself how lucky he was to have such a strong stomach, but his self-persuasion kept slipping. He forced himself to speak.

'The main thing is, doctor, can you find anything to confirm our suspicions that she was deliberately crashed in that Sunbeam? If not, we can all go home and forget it.'

The burly pathologist wagged his florid face.

'If she was, she must have been drunk, dead or unconscious. She wouldn't have sat there otherwise, would she?'

He bent over the body and began examining the outside in minute detail. Bray had been deputed to write down any dictated notes, and this helped to keep the young man's mind off the feelings of nausea which kept coming in waves from somewhere beneath his belt.

'Rigor mortis absent from all limbs ... lividity well marked on the back.'

Soames droned on as his fingers probed the pale flesh. The other police officers from the County looked on silently, each busy with their own thoughts or fighting their own particular brand of revulsion.

Every now and then Soames would ask for a photograph and the policemen from the photographic department would trundle up their tripod and scarify the mortuary with electronic flashes.

The doctor from London spent a long time probing around the head of the woman. He shaved off a wide area of the black hair and stepped back to let the camera team do their stuff again.

'Any joy, doctor?' asked Benbow cautiously. He had a lot of respect for the man's opinion, but knew from experience that he couldn't be stampeded into an opinion.

Eustace Soames rubbed his itching nose on his shoulder, his gloves already being fouled up.

'I don't like the look of it, Mr Benbow ... I'd like to have a look at the car afterwards.' He paused and pointed to the shaved area of the girl's head. 'There's a skin wound and a depressed fracture there. I can't tell much until I look under the skin, but it's most unlike a motor injury unless there's some unusual projection inside the car that would cause a deep narrow wound like that.'

Benbow's eyes glistened in his lumpy face. He forgot his stomach.

'It could be a blow from a weapon, you mean?'

Soames pursed his lips. 'Or a door handle or a window winder ... no, it's the wrong shape for those, too long.' As he spoke, he bent down so close to the week-old corpse that his big nose almost touched its left ear. Then he took fine-pointed forceps and carefully picked something from the edge of the head wound.

'Better have this, Inspector Hooper ... bit of fibre, may be a contact trace, unless it's something the undertakers left behind.'

The Yard laboratory officer stepped forward with a plastic envelope and delicately took the little yellow thread.

Soames turned his attention to the rest of the body and

65

looked at the fractures of the right arm and both legs. Then he began studying the inside of the forearms with greater care.

'See those marks there,' he said to Benbow, pointing to the insides of the elbows and arms. 'Needle marks. That one in the crook of the left elbow is direct into the vein. Looks much more recent than the others too.'

Archie Benbow had been too long in London's West End not to realise at once, the significance of the marks. 'So she was on the hook?' he said.

Soames nodded. 'Could explain why she was unconscious, I suppose, especially as that last one is intravenous instead of just under the skin like the others. Still, we're trying to run before we crawl, eh?'

The photographers moved away again and the bloody part of the business began.

For forty minutes the pathologist went through the organs, one by one. They were beginning to decay, but still good enough to show any abnormalities. He put several of them into big glass jars supplied by the laboratory officer and also took specimens of blood, urine, and stomach contents into bottles.

'Want some hair and fingernail clippings?' he asked the liaison officer.

'Aye, better have them, just for the record,' said Hooper. 'If she was put out forcibly by somebody, she may just have had the chance to run her nails down the skin of his face. God knows they're long enough!'

He collected the tips of Rita's scarlet nails into another bottle in the faint hope that enough flesh might be trapped under them to provide blood group identification.

Benbow noticed the doctor sniffed like a beagle when he came to slit open the stomach.

'Anything definite?'

'Pooh! Booze, plus-plus!' answered Eustace Soames, wrinkling his long nose. 'I don't know about drugs, but she's got enough alcohol in her belly to lay out an elephant!'

The examination finished about ten thirty, much to Bray's relief. Soames took the top of the skull away in a plastic bag, in case it was needed as an exhibit in the event of a court case. As he sat in the anteroom of the mortuary, he gave Benbow and Bray a summary of his findings.

'I think you've got a case, Mr Benbow. She's got gross injuries consistent with a motor crash: open fractures of both thighs, busted arm, her chest crushed from the steering wheel and a dislocated neck ... but I think she was dead before they occurred.'

The detective chief inspector bobbed his head gravely. Soames went on as he washed his hands and arms.

'She has a deep localised fracture on the left side of the skull ... most unlike a normal traffic injury, especially as the steering wheel has pinned her back so that her head couldn't ram the windscreen. Unless there's some odd projection inside the car to cause it, I don't see how the crash can be responsible.'

'You think it's a deliberate blow, then?'

Soames back-pedalled slightly.

'Ah well, the first thing a pathologist learns is never to say anything is impossible. But my opinion, for what it's worth, is that it's a blow. In court, any defence counsel worth his fee would tear me to shreds if I said that without any corroborating evidence.'

'Have we got any?' asked Benbow.

'Those leg injuries are very bad indeed – both main arteries torn across. Yet the sergeant here tells me that there wasn't much blood at the scene of the crash and certainly her kidneys and heart show not the slightest sign of severe haemorrhage. So I wouldn't be surprised if her circulation wasn't going when she hit the bridge – dead already, in fact.'

He made a final run-through with his comb in front of

the tiny mirror. 'And the last things, of course, are the alcohol and suspicion of drugs.'

Soames picked up his black instrument bag and made for the door.

'Let's have a look at this car then, shall we?'

The whole posse drove the mile to the police station and went round the back to where the wrecked Sunbeam was garaged.

As they walked across the yard, Benbow raised the question of the yellow thread. 'What's the significance of that?'

The forensic expert shrugged. 'Maybe nothing at all, but it was driven down from the surface into the scalp wound. It may be a contact trace for the thing that hit her, unless we find lots more of it in the car – upholstery fibre or some such thing.'

They reached the Sunbeam and clustered around it. Soames squinted inside and looked around the windscreen area.

'Nothing there – no fancy mirrors or spotlights sticking out. Anyway, it was too heavy a smack for anything flimsy like that to have caused the wound.'

'Any idea what it could have been?' hazarded Bray.

'Almost anything heavy – up to about an inch wide. Seems to have been a regular shape, but I can't say any more than that. There's more bullshine talked about the shape of blunt instruments than anything else in this game!'

Bray had wandered around to the back of the Alpine and was peering into the open boot. The crash had so distorted the bodywork that the lid was jammed wide open.

'What about this?' he called.

The others joined him and he pointed to a wheel brace lying loose in the back.

Soames shook his head. 'Too big and too round ... it

would have punched a bigger hole than we've got ... but that might do.'

He indicated the long, slim starting handle clipped into supports near the spare wheel.

Hooper bent down to look more closely at it.

'Nothing to see but you never know ... I'll take it and the brace, just for the laughs.' He slid the two metal tools into large plastic bags, taking care not to disturb any prints or foreign material on the shafts.

The party soon broke up, Eustace Soames to his Saturday golf and the police to their homes.

On the way back to London, the keen young Bray challenged his boss. 'Well, sir, have we or have we not got a murder on our hands?'

Soames sat regally back in the police Wolseley, his podgy hands folded in his lap. 'I think so, lad, I feel it in me bones. But a lot will depend on you, Jimmy.' He turned his head to Hooper, sitting alongside him. 'If you find blood on those tools, or if you find enough booze or drugs in her blood to make it obvious that she was too far gone to have been able to drive, then we're away.'

'When will we know that?'

Jimmy Hooper scratched his nose thoughtfully.

'Weekend now ... I expect someone will do the stains and fibres part of it for you, but the analysis will have to wait till Monday. We're working flat out as it is, but this lot will get priority.'

'And until then, Bray me boy, I think we'll have a gentle little snoop around Soho ... tomorrow morning as soon as the pubs open will be about right, I think.'

Chapter Seven

About ten thirty that night, when Conrad Draper and Irish entered the Nineties Club, Snigger was perspiring behind his bar, dealing with the peak of the Saturday night rush.

He had no particular reason to take any notice of the pair; they were both members and so far, nothing had cropped up to tie them in with the tape recorder affair which Paul had eventually confided to Snigger.

The two men parked themselves at the end of the bar and began drinking. When the rush eased off an hour later, Snigger had time to take more notice of the clients.

The first cabaret had finished and the late one was due at midnight. His eye passed over the line of faces at the bar and only paused fleetingly on Irish.

He wondered idly whether the man had really given up the drug game or whether he was still an undisclosed competitor. He had only been a small-time dealer – a 'ten deck man' – and the barman had not heard that he was active lately.

Snigger had already got rid of about fifty parcels of heroin and cocaine that evening. He kept a special stock of cigarettes in a separate glass cupboard behind the bar, which the two barmaids were forbidden to touch. In each of the packets he had a little polythene envelope of drugs hidden beneath the silver foil.

When one of his regular customers came up and asked for twenty cigarettes – 'You know, my usual brand' – they got one from the private stock. In exchange, they passed over a pound note and even the closest observer would fail to see that Snigger dropped only a few small coins back in their palms as an apology for change. Some of his regulars, who were on big doses, passed over fivers and got special packets handed back with correspondingly large drug packets.

Snigger's only mental comment as his eye roved on to Conrad was that it was about time he had a decent win on the horses. He had poured hundreds of pounds into Draper's pockets and in spite of his experience as an ex-jockey, had had very little in return.

I'll bet I've bought him half a dozen like that, he thought grudgingly, eyeing the expensive but flashily-cut suit that hung from Draper's wide shoulders.

Conrad Draper suddenly looked up and caught the barman's eye. He raised a massive finger and crooked it in an imperious summons.

Snigger walked slowly down the bar, rapidly totting up his recent gambling losses. By the time he got to the far end he had calculated that he should be free of any debts with Draper, so this must be about something else.

The bookie grinned falsely in greeting.

'Hi, Snigger, how's tricks? Give me whisky and soda and have something yourself.'

Snigger served them and poured a beer for himself. He wondered what this ingratiating overture was leading up to, as normally Draper ignored him.

'Snigger, has Mr Golding been in lately?'

Conrad, with a pathetic attempt at nonchalance slung the question straight across the net.

Snigger, poker-faced, but seething with interest inside, shook his head. He instinctively felt that something was going to break that might be worth a handful of fivers to him.

'Sorry, Mr Draper, haven't noticed him since last weekend.' He slid the drinks aside to wipe the bar, looking at Draper's taut expression from under lowered lids.

'Not a sign of him?' Conrad persisted.

'No ... I heard about Miss Ronalde's accident ... awful, eh? Perhaps that'll keep him away from here for a bit. In here he met her, see.'

A shadow passed across Conrad's face that was not lost on the astute barman. He began to see the light, fringed with gold guineas.

'Where can I find Golding?' Draper spoke gruffly now, any pretence at casual conversation gone.

'Sorry, Mr Draper, haven't the faintest. Think he lives out of town most of the time.'

'Where? You must know. I know you're pretty thick with him.'

There was anger and pure menace in the ex-wrestler's voice now.

'I don't. He comes and goes but I don't ask questions. I wouldn't last long in this job if I did.'

Draper half-rose and leaned across the bar.

'You won't last bloody long as it is, if you don't come clean.' He whispered in a stage voice that made the customers on each side of him look around in surprise and alarm.

Irish, more alive to the risks of making their business too public, tugged ineffectually at Draper's jacket.

'Lay off, boss, you can't grill him here.'

Draper glared at the barman for a moment then subsided onto his stool. 'Look, Snigger, there's a few quid in it for you if you tell me how to get in touch with him. I just want to talk some business with him, see.'

Gigal lied with easy fluency.

'I would if I could, Mr Draper, but I just can't help you. He usually comes in here about every fortnight, so he's not due till the end of the week at the earliest.'

'Haven't you got a forwarding address, damn you?'

Snigger contrived to look shocked.

'I don't have addresses of customers, sir ... why should I?'

Draper's patience went again. He stretched his big arm across the bar and jabbed Snigger in the chest with an iron finger.

'I've heard you and Golding are pretty close. If you come across with his address, there's twenty in it for you, see. Otherwise, I'll suddenly find that you haven't paid for a lot of your bets and send a couple of boys over to bounce you – good and hard – get it?'

The amount of venom that he got over in such a low voice impressed even Snigger, but he stuck his ground.

'I'm sorry, but I can't help you. God knows where he goes to when he leaves here. I'll give him a message if he comes in – what shall I tell him you want to talk about?' Conrad sank back again.

'Nothing … you keep your trap shut or I'll come and knock you silly. If he comes in, ring me up pronto, understand?'

He threw back his drink and got up suddenly. With a sign to Irish to stay where he was, he strode off towards the back of the club.

'Nice fellow,' said Snigger bitterly. 'Buys me a drink and then offers to belt my head off. What's eating him?'

Irish, who was almost awash with neat brandy, shook his head mournfully. 'He's mad keen to get hold of this Golding character.'

Snigger saw his chance to do a bit more snooping.

'What for? I hardly know the bloke – only that he used to bring his fancy woman in here for a booze-up and a bit of a hop.'

Irish had been hitting the bottle heavily all day and this, together with fellow-feeling for Snigger as another underdog, made him a little incautious with his tongue.

'I dunno, ever since he heard about that Rita dame getting the chop, he's been damn near chewing the carpet in temper.' Irish's voice was thick and slurred, and Snigger tried to push him a little further.

'Was he jealous or something?' he asked, in the right combination of lewdness and offhandedness that would appeal to the Irishman.

'Ay, maybe he was after being that way,' mumbled O'Keefe, his accent more pronounced than ever. 'Though bints is ten-a-penny to Conrad. I don't see why he should get so sweated up about this one. He's only been knocking her off for a few weeks.'

Snigger almost heard the jangle of cash registers in his brain as Irish let this drop. Unfortunately, the man seemed to realise that he had said too much and in spite of Snigger's persuasion, he refused to say any more.

Meanwhile, Draper had pushed his way round the edge of the crowded dance floor and reached the stage. He climbed up and went through the side entrance into the corridor and then to Silver's room.

He barged in without knocking and slammed the door behind him. Ray Silver was stooping over a large safe set in the wall behind his desk, busily putting cardboard boxes into a suitcase.

The club owner had taken fright ever since rumours about Rita's death had filtered through to him. Coupling this with Golding and the drug trade, he had had a sudden desire to clear out any incriminating evidence in the shape of heroin, cocaine, and morphine from his premises.

As the betting shop king burst in, he whirled around with a scared expression clamped to his face. He tried to slam the safe door shut, but relaxed when he saw who his visitor was.

'Draper! What's the idea? This is a private office,' he blustered in an attempt to recover his poise.

Conrad outclassed him without difficulty. He walked to Silver's chair, dropped into it, and put his feet on the desk while he felt for one of his loathsome cigars. It was pure Chicago-ese and Draper savoured every second.

'Shaddup!' he began conversationally. Silver opened

his mouth and then shut it again like a plump goldfish. He could find no suitable words. He looked uncertainly at his unwelcome guest and then at the big steel safe. Eventually he slammed the heavy door shut and came to stand opposite Conrad, the desk between them.

'What d'you want?' he demanded in a quavering, reedy voice. 'You surely can't want more fixes already?'

Conrad spoke evenly. 'Nope, I don't want your junk.'

He picked a shred of tobacco from his cold cigar and went on.

'I just want to know where you get it.'

Ray Silver sat down on a hard chair opposite Draper. He smiled nervously.

'Now look, Conrad, you know how it is. If I grassed on my supplier, he'd cut me off dead – and that means you wouldn't get any more.'

It was a weak argument and he knew it.

'Nuts! You're not the only punter in the street, not by a hell of a long way.'

Silver looked baffled.

'What's the idea, you trying to get in on the racket or something?'

The idea of a strong-arm man turned bookie trying to muscle in on his brand of graft made the worm turn a little and his tone became belligerent.

Draper waved his hands over the desk in an attitude of submission.

'All right, I'll come clean.' He spat out his cigar and lit a cigarette. 'I already know where you get your stuff ... it's from Golding, isn't it?'

Silver stared woodenly at him, but Conrad carried on without waiting for an answer.

'I want to find him ... it's urgent. I don't want to cut into your racket – piddling little trade after mine,' he added grandly. He flicked his ash onto the Eurasian's desk top. 'No, you can keep your pep pill business, Silver, all I want is Golding. And you're going to help me find him.'

The proprietor, relieved to hear that Draper was not after his trade, grinned fawningly across at the bookie.

'I'd tell you in a flash, Conrad, square I would, only I don't know myself. I've been trying to find out this evening – I'm getting worried about my supplies, if he doesn't show up after that business with that bloody woman.'

Draper scowled furiously. 'Come off it, slant-eyes! Don't mess me around.'

Silver held his hands out appealingly.

'God strike me, Conrad, I'm telling the truth. I don't know how to reach him … no address, no phone number, nothing!'

He fidgeted in front of the desk.

'I heard a squeak today that the narks are wondering about that accident. I don't know what it means, but whatever it is, it don't sound healthy. That's why I'm unloading my stuff.'

He jerked his head at the suitcase lying near the safe.

Draper slowly leaned across the desk and then slammed a great fist onto the centre of the polished top.

'I don't bleeding well believe you, you damn liar! Your barman has just given me the same patter. You're trying to tell me that you do business with a guy for years, he comes in here regularly and yet you don't know where to find him?'

Silver stood cracking his finger joints in agitation.

'It's the truth, Draper, honest. I got an idea he lives out of London – he said something once about having a train to catch … he had that flat in Newman Street, of course.' The Eurasian ended brightly, as if this was likely to be great news to Conrad.

Draper leered sarcastically at him. 'Big deal, I can read the bloody newspapers as well as you.'

He stood up and deliberately dropped his lighted

cigarette onto the thick fitted carpet. Ray Silver watched it burn a hole without daring to protest.

'I'll give you till Monday night to get your memory back, greaseball,' grated Conrad in pure Mickey Spillane speech. 'Then if you can't do better than tonight, I'll arrange to have the decorations in your club altered a bit – my boys are good at that.'

He stalked out, ignoring the whining of the club owner, who followed him to the end of the passage still babbling excuses.

Silver went back to his office and opened the safe again. He took out a small automatic pistol and handling it with the nervousness of a novice, slipped it into the side pocket of his dinner jacket.

Chapter Eight

There was a lull in the affair for the first couple of days of the new week.

Benbow started to move the machinery of formal investigation into the contacts of Rita Ronalde, the divisional detectives and Sergeant Bray going out into the Newman Street area to follow up the few obvious leads given by the cleaning woman and local garages.

But late on the Sunday night, a prostitute was strangled in an alley behind Poland Street and much of the police effort was diverted to catching the suspect. Even when this was settled twenty-four hours later, there was little that Benbow could do until he had the reports from the Yard laboratory.

At the Nineties Club there was also a period of uneasy waiting. In spite of his threat, Conrad did not turn up with his hoodlums on the Monday night, but at lunchtime the next day, when Silver was eating a huge spaghetti bolognese at his favourite trattoria. A tall and evil-looking Italian sauntered over and stood at his table.

He waited until Silver had a forkful of food almost at his mouth then jogged his elbow so that a couple of yards of the pasta fell into the club owner's lap.

Silver looked up angrily, an oath on his lips. It froze there as he recognised Luigi, one of Conrad's sidekicks.

Luigi leered down at the podgy Eurasian.

'Draper said for me to tell you,' he said in a throaty Neapolitan accent, 'He's coming around tonight – so you gotta be a good boy, eh?'

He picked up the salt cellar, pulled the top off, and

emptied the whole contents into the middle of Silver's meal. Then he laughed and sauntered out into the street.

The waiters, fellow countrymen of his, had watched the whole performance but, whether from fear or approval, made no attempt to interfere.

Silver cleaned himself up as best he could, then walked back to the Nineties. As he trotted through the streets, cold anger stung his waspish little mind into schemes for revenge.

He wondered what was behind this sudden interest of Draper's in Paul Golding. He himself had spoken nothing but the truth about his ignorance of the dope smuggler's whereabouts. That made this present persecution all the harder to bear.

'What the hell am I to tell him tonight? The bloody man is plain crazy!' Revenge took second place to anxiety as he padded down Gerrard Street. Everything he had was tied up in the club. He had recently ploughed all his profits from the narcotics business into having the premises lavishly redecorated, to attract the better class of customer – and addict.

He knew that in a few minutes of rough stuff, he would lose both the decorations of the place and the more important goodwill of the clients, who wanted peace and anonymity to conduct their affairs.

He failed to see where Conrad Draper fitted into the Golding scheme. He knew that the betting shop boss took small doses of heroin. Was it conceivable that he was trying to break into the selling game himself?

Draper had a ready-made system of distribution in his chain of gambling offices all over the West End, and Irish O'Keefe had some experience of pushing the stuff. But it seemed all wrong, this approach. He would hardly burst in on what would be his closest rival and demand to meet the wholesaler in such a violent way.

Everyone knew that Draper was a bit touched – if he

had been a boxer and not a wrestler in the past, Silver would have put it down to being punch-drunk. But there must be something else going on, something important enough to make Draper threaten him with the treatment usually reserved for the Soho protection rackets.

By the time the half-caste owner had mulled all this over, his short, quick footsteps had brought him to the closed door of the Nineties. He let himself in with his key and found the lights already lit on the staircase.

His heart gave a bound and he stopped to listen, afraid that Draper's louts had already arrived. But the distant clink of bottles from below reassured him. It was Snigger doing his weekly bar stock account.

Downstairs, all the chairs were up on the tables and the harsh lights reserved for the cleaners were full on.

Gigal was dressed in a roll-necked sweater, a legacy of his days on the turf, instead of his Victorian get-up.

'Hello, Mr Silver, you're in early. What's happened to your suit?'

As soon as the owner had opened his overcoat, the remains of the spaghetti were all too evident. Ray Silver told him bitterly of the incident in the trattoria.

'What the hell am I going to tell Draper tonight? If I don't pitch him some yarn, he'll have those yobs of his around here before we close. And if I do spin a pack of lies to satisfy him for tonight, he'll soon find the truth and come beating me up tomorrow.'

He stalked up and down, beating a fist into his open hand.

'I'm going to be ruined, Snigger. One punch-up in here with an audience and that's my lot – I'd have to close up.'

Snigger scratched his head with a pencil.

'I wish Golding would turn up – let him do the worrying,' he said, with complete honesty.

He badly wanted to get in touch with Golding himself,

to tell him of the developments that made it almost certain that Conrad Draper was the man whose voice Paul had heard on the hidden tape recorder.

'Think Draper's boys really will come tonight?'

Snigger shrugged. 'Gawd knows – if he wanted to do a real good smudge job on you he'd send them late at night when the place is full up.'

The Eurasian looked sick with anxiety. His round moon face was bleached with worry and his slightly slanted eyes glistened.

Snigger was struck by an idea. 'Tell you what, if you'll risk it and don't mind forking out a few quid ...'

He took a few minutes to outline his plan and at the end of it the club owner was on the point of swooning with undiluted fear.

'If it goes wrong, Draper will kill me ... you know what he's like ... mad as they come, thinks he's some sort of Al Capone.'

'You're going to catch a packet in any case,' shrugged Snigger indifferently. 'A big shindig here and the regulars will be off like a shot. They come here to enjoy a bit of peace and quiet with other people's wives, but there's plenty of other clubs waiting to take their custom.'

He was also about to mention the loss of the drug racket, but stopped himself just in time. He wasn't supposed to know.

'OK, OK, we'll do it ... what'll it cost?'

Desperation drove Silver into accepting Snigger's last ditch scheme.

'About a hundred quid, all told ... and cheap at the price,' the barman reassured him.

After they had fixed the details of the plot, Snigger went back to his bar stock and finished his totting-up of the liquor sales.

About five o'clock, he pulled on his raincoat and made his way up Tottenham Court Road to Ferber Street, which was really one side of a Bloomsbury square.

On the third floor of a block of flats, he halted at a door which had a blank space alongside the bell push. Snigger rang half-heartedly, being certain that Golding would not be there. After a moment's silence had confirmed this, he took out a sheet of paper and a ballpoint and wrote a hasty message. He slipped it under the door, gave a last futile peal on the bell, and walked back to the automatic lift.

Having done his best to give his senior partner as much warning as possible, the ex-jockey went home to his bachelor flat above the Queen of Scots public house in Fulham, to get ready for the evening stint in the Nineties.

Chapter Nine

Conrad Draper lolled in the back seat of his immense American Ford as Irish drove him slowly down Gerrard Street. He rolled his unlit cigar to one corner of his mouth and spat orders through the other.

'Drop me now, then go back for the others – an' don't be all night about it. Park the barrow and come straight to the club.'

'Luigi and Harry ain't got membership cards,' objected Irish.

Draper swore at the small-mindedness of his lieutenant.

'For God's sake, this isn't a courtesy call – if the flunkey on the door opens his trap, ram your fist down it. I should be in the bar when you come, but if I'm not, come straight through to the office at the back and no stopping off for a crafty booze on the way.'

The car drew up and the doorman of the Nineties hurried across the pavement to open the door for him to get out.

'It's half eleven now,' said Conrad as a parting shot to Irish. 'So get back here inside five or ten minutes.'

The car, looking like a spaceship on four white-walled tyres, glided away and the turf tycoon went down into the club.

The doorman hurried to his house telephone and pressed the button marked Office. He spoke in an urgent whisper, though there was no one to overhear.

'He's just come in, Mr Silver ... yes, on his own.'

Snigger watched the large figure of the ex-wrestler stride past the bar and heard the line of protests as he marched unheedingly over feet and against tables in the gloom. The lights were down as the cabaret was in progress. The sultry blonde was crooning away, but Conrad, oblivious of everything but his mobster reputation, forged on towards the stage.

For a moment his broad silhouette was outlined alongside the slinky singer as he clambered up on to the platform. He vanished through the side door in the wings and groped his way up the corridor to Silver's office door, which showed a sliver of light beneath the panels.

Without any pretence of knocking, he barged in and stood blinking in the light of the desk lamp which had been deliberately turned towards the door to blind him. The other lights in the room were out and he felt a sudden surge of alarm.

'Hey – what the hell?'

His arms were suddenly seized and he was dragged into the centre of the room. Simultaneously, the lights came on and the door was slammed shut.

The astounded bookie found himself held in a vice-like grip by two large and ugly men. They lugged him to the desk, where a pale but shakily triumphant Ray Silver stood waiting.

Conrad fell to swearing, more out of rage than fear. His American façade gave way to the more descriptive language of Stepney and Whitechapel as he ran through his repertoire of blistering obscenity.

The thugs gave him a moment or two to let off steam then one of them wrenched his elbow violently.

'Shut yer gob!' he growled expressively.

Conrad nearly exploded in a shower of outraged blood and flesh. No one had spoken to him like that for nearly ten years.

'I'll cut you to little pieces for this,' he rampaged, 'I'll bloody kill you … you … smash you …'

He ran out of words bad enough to express his feelings

and ended with a sob of frustrated rage, his face purple with emotion. He failed to recognise either of the toughs as local men and tried to soothe his shattered pride by telling himself that they couldn't possibly know who he was. He started to put that right as soon as the thought entered his head. Draper snarled at the two men who were stoically hanging on to his writhing arms.

'You don't know who I am, eh ... you better find out quick!

'Yes, butch ... we know all about that ... you're Draper the Chicago Kid. That don't cut no ice with us,' growled the first man, who looked as if he used concrete as an aftershave lotion. 'Now shurrup and listen to the man over there.'

He gave another excruciating twist to Conrad's elbow. The ex-wrestler realised from experience that he had no hope of breaking their hold.

Ray Silver did not share his opinion. He kept his hand on the automatic in his jacket pocket and when he had the chance to speak, he lugged it out. Using it to boost his shaky nerves, he pointed it waveringly in the direction of Conrad's navel.

The bookie's jaw dropped when he saw the gun. Even his gangster complex hadn't driven him as far as carrying a gun around with him. He had earned a year's corrective training in his youth for being found in illegal possession of a pistol and this had encouraged him to keep clear of them ever since. To see the Eurasian pointing one at him now was a physical shock.

'Silver, you must be cracked! What y'doing with a rod?'

The club owner began to speak. His first attempt was a high-pitched squeak but he tried again and managed to make a tremendous croak.

'You started it, Draper – you and your ideas about busting up my club.'

'I'll eat you alive, you little squirt,' roared Conrad. 'What the hell are you up to? And stop pointing that damn shooter at me.'

'I want to know why you're so interested in Golding.' The club owner's confidence increased as he saw how powerless Draper was in the hands of the two thugs.

Conrad's blood pressure had come down a little by now after the first shock had worn off. He had not the slightest trace of fear; nothing could happen to the great, the invincible Conrad – nothing like what was going to happen to Silver and his bunch of amateurs as soon as Irish and the boys got here. He began reasoning with the half-caste, partly to pass the time away.

'Now be sensible, Ray … tell your yobs to take their hands off me and slide away. I'll forget the hard words we had about roughing your place up. All I want to know is where to find Golding.'

'And I tell you I don't know. Can't you get that into your thick head?'

'All right, now put that rod away, it might go off accidentally – you wouldn't want to be topped just because your finger slipped, would you?'

Ray Silver shook his head emphatically. Now that he was in the saddle, he wanted to stay there. The internal telephone rang urgently but he ignored it to concentrate on Conrad.

'Come on, tell me – why do you want Golding so badly? Are you trying to cut in on the peddling game?'

Conrad gave another experimental shrug to his arms, but they were held as if in a vice. The two men stood impassively at his side, apparently bored by the whole proceedings.

'Tell these punks to scram and I'll talk to you,' he grated.

Silver shook his head. 'You do the talking from there. You're in no position to bargain.'

He was wrong. For the second time in a few minutes, the door burst open and Harry and Luigi erupted into the room. They stared around for a split second and then jumped at the thugs that held Conrad. These two promptly let go of his arms to defend themselves and the bookie hurled himself at the desk.

He brought his fist down in a great chop which pinned Silver's wrist to the desktop and sent the gun spinning across the floor.

While the four heavyweights were mixing it in the middle of the room, Conrad was belabouring the Eurasian about the head with the flat of his hand. Silver rapidly slid to the floor and lay blubbering with fright and pain. Conrad scooped up the automatic and turned his attention to the main battle.

Big Harry and his opponent were about evenly matched and were slugging away as if they were enjoying it. The second, a burly fellow with a scarred face, had Luigi in a half-nelson and was hammering his left kidney into a fine pulp.

Conrad stuffed the pistol into his pocket, got a professional wrestling hold on the man and dropped him clean onto his head on the floor, where he passed out cold. The other thug saw this from the comer of his eye and promptly dodged for the door before Conrad had a chance to repeat the treatment on him.

Unfortunately for Irish O'Keefe, the escaping man met him in the corridor outside and gave him a tremendous thump in the chest as he made his getaway. Harry dragged Irish inside and dumped him in a chair to recover.

'What the hell kept you?' demanded Conrad, breathing heavily and restoring his oily waves with a comb. Irish gasped while he tried to get his lungs working again and Harry had to explain for him.

'He stopped to show the doorman his razor – the guy was trying to use the house phone.'

Conrad grunted and went to look behind the desk at the fallen owner. He was still lying on the floor, moaning and trying to look mortally injured, but a flash of his shifty eyes told Conrad that he was shamming.

'Get up – we got talking to do.'

The pasty-faced man dragged himself slowly to his feet and pulled his dishevelled dinner jacket together. He was shivering like someone with malaria. Conrad pulled out the Webley and took careful aim at Silver's stomach. The club owner screamed. 'Please – no!'

Conrad laughed and, leaning forwards, prodded him hard with the blunt muzzle.

'All right, you double-crossing little creep, I'm not going to perforate you – yet!' He raised a hand and gave the other a resounding slap across the cheeks, which were already swollen and bruised.

Silver yelped and began to sob.

'Shut up – you're breaking my heart. Now you can see you're not in the same class as the big boys – stick to snow peddling and your song and dance acts.'

Harry interrupted to ask what they should do with the other bruiser who was just regaining consciousness.

'Take him round the front and dump him in the street – he should have learnt his lesson like slit-eyes here.'

Harry and Luigi dragged the body away and Conrad put the automatic back into his pocket.

'Look, Silver, I want to know the minute Golding shows up here or as soon as you hear anything from him – see?'

Silver nodded mutely

'He must show up soon,' went on Conrad in his mood of expansive forgiveness, he's got to flog his stuff to someone or starve. And when he does, you get on the blower to me as fast as your fat legs'll carry you – see?'

Silver saw and nodded and gulped eagerly.

'But why – what's the game?' he cringed.

The bookie seemed to swell before Silver's eyes.

'The bastard croaked my dame – and I'm going to get him for it.'

He pulled out the pistol and began playing with it.

'I'm going to kill him when I catch up with him.'

Ray looked with fascination at the Webley.

'But the police ... they said it was an accident.'

'Yeah – so why are they nosing about asking questions today?'

'You got no proof that Golding had anything to do with it!' objected Silver, getting bolder now that the brunt of Draper's anger had been deflected onto Golding.

Conrad tossed the gun carelessly from one hand to the other.

'No, not yet. That's where you come in. I want to talk to Golding – by the time I've finished with him I'll know everything I want to know.'

He suddenly poked the gun right into the Eurasian's face.

Ray backed away hastily.

'I think he's got some sort of legit business somewhere – probably outside London. Does he know you're on to him?'

Draper waved the automatic dangerously.

'He knows somebody's on to him – but he doesn't know who – and you're not going to tell him, are you? You wouldn't want to come to a sticky end, Silver.'

The viciousness in the last words cut like a knife as Draper wheeled around and went to the door. He turned again in the opening for a last word, in true Bowery style.

'Get me on the blower the minute you hear – and remember, chum, you're living on borrowed time until I get Golding.'

He strode away down the corridor, followed by Irish, who still grunted with pain every time he breathed.

Silver stared blankly at his writing pad, seeing nothing

but trouble written there.

Inspector Turnbull came down from the laboratory on the top of the new building of Scotland Yard and crossed over into the dingy red-brick monstrosity that housed many of the senior officers. He found Archie Benbow's room and squeezed into it, clutching a sheaf of papers.

'Good job you haven't got a cat, Archie, you couldn't swing the damn thing in here.'

Bray was toiling at a big filing cabinet that seemed to fill half the room and Benbow was staring out of the window. He swung round to greet the liaison officer.

'Hi, George ... you're damn right about this place.' He waved aggrievedly towards the window. 'In all these TV plays, the detective has a lovely view of the river and the County Hall from his spacious apartment,' he complained. 'All I've got is the blank wall of an alley leading to Cannon Row.'

Bray looked up and grinned. 'Oh, I don't know, sir – if you lean out far enough, you can see the toilets on the comer quite plainly.'

Turnbull waved the papers he held.

'Got some results on the Laskey woman,' he announced. Bray slammed his cabinet shut and came to stand at Benbow's elbow as the Admiral sank down behind his desk. Turnbull drew up a chair, which just about used up all the remaining space in the room. He was a tall thin, perpetually pipe-smoking man, never in a flap, but always intent on getting on with the job with the least possible fuss.

'She had a load of alcohol in her, as we expected,' he began, 'the blood level was three hundred and twenty milligrams per cent – getting on towards the coma level – if she wasn't absolutely dead to the world, she'd have been so groggy that she wouldn't have cared if she'd been coshed with forty starting handles!'

Benbow's beady eyes flashed. 'Ah-hah! The handle ... you got anything definite on that?'

'Yes, Archie, we've come up trumps with it.'

Turnbull dived into a large envelope and came out with some glossy prints.

'We've compared some of the fibres caught on the rusty part of the handle with samples from several samples of yellow household dusters and the sort they sell for cleaning cars. Several of them correspond exactly with the strands on the handle and with the fibres that the pathologist picked from the girl's head wound.'

'That doesn't prove that she was hit with that particular handle,' objected Benbow.

'No, I agree, but it all helps,' said Turnbull.

'Can you narrow down the source of the particular fibres?' asked Bray.

'No, the dusters are sold all over the place – Halfords and Woolworths, that kind of shop.'

'So it doesn't help one damn bit,' snarled Benbow. Turnbull ground his teeth on the stem of his pipe.

'Wait a bit, wait a bit – there's more to come yet ... blood, glorious blood.'

He lit his pipe with infuriating slowness and spoke again through a barrage of blue smoke. 'The knuckle of that handle looked clean enough – it had probably been wiped over with a wet rag – perhaps the same or a similar yellow duster. But the steel still gave a strong positive benzidine reaction for blood It's hellishly sensitive – will pick up about one part in three million. This handle crank gave a whacking strong positive. Then they used some fancy tests on the rust scrapings in case it was just the iron giving a false reaction, but it was still a bonanza.'

'What then?' asked Benbow, always a little suspicious of the scientist's expertise.

'The boys upstairs used the usual grouping techniques and this new mixed agglutination test to show that the

ABO and MN groups were the same on the handle and the specimen from the post-mortem on Laskey. She was group A, not that it matters to you.'

Benbow digested this. 'Does that mean she was definitely hit by that handle and no other?'

Turnbull shook his head. 'No ... have a heart, Archie; we're workers, not wizards. But it means that that handle was dipped in human group A blood at some time, and it's hardly likely to be anyone else, is it, considering she's got a hole in her head the exact shape of the said bit of metal.'

'Got anything else?' grunted Benbow.

'Soames has had another look at the fracture and agrees that the starting handle would do very nicely for the offending weapon. He says that she must have been hit from the left side, so that almost certainly means she was in the passenger seat when her killer took a swipe at her.'

'Why?'

'The pathologist says – and I agree with him – that if she was in the driving seat, the murderer couldn't get a good enough swing to fetch her such a smack as that ... the roof of the car would be in the way, it would be too cramped altogether. Looks as if he got her stinking drunk, opened the door on the nearside, and whacked her from there. The yellow fibres were some from a car duster when he attempted to clean a bit of the blood up – or perhaps he put it over the head before he socked her. That would be more like it, it would explain why there were fibres deep in the wound and why there was so little blood matted on the hair.'

'Charming ... I bet you think up lovely bedtime stories for your kids, chum,' said Benbow dryly.

Turnbull grinned.

'She couldn't have been driving anyway ... I defy any slim young dame to control a car for a hundred yards with a blood alcohol of three twenty ... she'd have been flat out, snoring her head off.'

Benbow beamed. 'Ain't science bloody marvellous, Bray?'

The fresh-faced sergeant nodded obediently.

'So there's no doubt about our having a murder on the books, sir ... we can pull out all the stops to try to get some sense out of the yobs around the top end of Dean Street.'

Benbow's smile faded. 'Huh – some hope. We can pound those streets till our feet show through the soles of our boots, and not get so much as the time of day.'

Turnbull puffed away calmly.

'You still haven't heard it all: she had a load of drugs in her as well as the hooch.'

Benbow looked up sharply. 'Hard stuff?'

'Heroin.'

'Those marks on her arms were the real thing, then,' said Bray.

Turnbull grinned. 'Yes, lad – and she wasn't a diabetic having insulin injections, as you suggested at the time.'

He opened a folder and looked at a copy of Soames' post-mortem report.

'The most recent injection mark was into the main vein in the left arm – had a little blob of clotted blood on it, so it probably was only a few hours old when she died – looks as if she had a mainliner soon before she was killed. All the others were just under the skin.'

Benbow nodded thoughtfully.

'Filled up with grog, then drugged and finally beaten over the head ... nice company she kept!'

He riffled through the documents that Turnbull had produced then slapped the desk with a dumpy fist.

'We've got to find this bastard; he's in the professional class. He kills when it suits his book, not on impulse.'

'Where's the motive?' asked Turnbull, calmly sucking his pipe.

Benbow threw up his arms dramatically.

'God knows, but where there are drugs, there's crime … every one in the book. I'll lay an even fiver with you that the narcotics angle comes into this somewhere.'

Bray was looking as chirpy as a schoolboy.

'What about the Drugs Squad? Shall I nip over and have a natter to them, sir?'

The department known loosely as the Drugs Squad was more accurately the Narcotics Office, a small group of detective sergeants whose main job was to regulate the proper usage of dangerous drugs and make spot checks on druggists' and manufacturers' records. But apart from this, they held a considerable interest in all forms of importation, both legal and otherwise and had a close link with the Customs people over the problem of smuggling.

Benbow bobbed his jowls in agreement. 'May as well, lad. They've got their own contacts, something might turn up. We're never going to get any joy out of that bunch of yobs up the street.' He jerked a thumb in the general direction of Soho.

Turnbull hauled himself out of his chair.

'Any good trying to trace where she got her dope?'

Benbow looked glum. 'Just a few decks? There are a hundred places in the West End where she could have got them. Still, Bray can see what the narcotics boys can suggest.'

Turnbull turned to go back to his scientific wonderland upstairs.

'The lads are going over the dust and other stuff from the car for contact traces – if anything comes of it I'll give you a shout.'

After he had gone, Bray went back to finish his filing and Benbow mournfully thumbed through the thin folder on Rita Laskey.

'There's something about this one that gives me the creeps,' he muttered. 'Too damn cold-blooded – the chap that did this has killed before, I'll bet – and he'll kill again as soon as it suits him.'

Paul Jacobs made a different entry into London on the following Friday afternoon. He came by train to Paddington as before, the typical provincial businessman. But this time there was none of the toilet and left-luggage routine. He intended to keep clear of Soho for the time being, so he openly took a taxi to his Ferber Street flat.

He got to his door without seeing a soul except the taxi driver. Once inside, he was as effectively insulated from London as he had been in Cardiff. There was no cleaning woman to pester him and he was delightfully alone.

The envelope on the mat told him that Snigger had been there; no one else knew of the place. He went into the kitchen and made some coffee while he read and digested the contents of the barman's message. They disturbed him considerably and he paced the room uneasily, trying to fit this new information into his plans for the coming weekend.

'Conrad Draper, I – I've heard of him but never laid eyes on him as far as I know,' he muttered to himself. 'I've got to know more about this.'

He went to the telephone in the lounge and rang the landlord of the Queen of Scots in Fulham.

Twenty minutes later, a taxi dropped the ex-jockey outside and he hurried up to Jacobs' flat.

'I'm in a spot,' admitted Paul, after he had settled Snigger down with a glass and a bottle of whisky. 'I've got to get the orders for this weekend; I'm off to Germany tomorrow.'

'You've grown a moustache, then,' observed the barman.

During the ten days he had been away, Paul had allowed a fair military-style line of hair to grow on his upper lip. It was some help in altering his appearance.

'That ain't going be half enough disguise if you're

thinking of showing your face around Soho,' added Snigger.

'Why – only this Draper is looking for me, isn't he?'

'I hear tell that the police have been asking around a bit since last Saturday. Nothing much at first, but there's a steady bit of questioning going on. They took the cleaner from Newman Street in for questioning and a few of the tradespeople from around that part.'

Paul pondered this carefully. 'Heard any reason why? Your grapevine usually knows everything.'

Snigger shook his head.

'The dicks have been real canny about this one. They've had their hands full of other things this week. A tom got croaked and there were another two bank jobs pulled. But they haven't dropped a whisper yet about the Rita business.'

He looked up sharply at the other man, his bright Cockney eyes questioning.

'Did you rub her out, Mr Golding?' he asked quietly. 'I know she helped put the black on you with Draper, so she had it coming. You can tell me, you know, my mouth is tight enough.'

Paul looked down at him for a moment then nodded abruptly. He trusted Snigger more than anyone, and needed him as an ally more than ever, now things were going to be more difficult.

'Yes, Snigger, I fixed her. I had to – she had got dangerous. It was nothing personal, but she had to go.'

He paused, stared absently into his glass then told the barman the whole story.

'So you see, Paul Golding can't exist any more. I'm Paul Harrap from now on. I'm going to lay low for a bit, then work up a new front for myself when I get back from the next trip – take another flat, build up a whole new identity for myself.'

'What about the club?' asked the ex-jockey. 'Are you

laying off there?'

'I'll have to go this once to get Silver's order … after that I'll avoid it like the plague. You'll have to do the go-between business for me where Silver is concerned.'

'Where are you going tomorrow – Brussels again?'

'No, Munich this trip.' Paul Jacobs wearily smoothed back the hair from his forehead. He felt like chucking the whole game up and going straight back to his nice comfortable house, his placid wife and his genuine antique trade.

But he knew he never would. The little devil deep inside him would always prod him into just one more venture and he couldn't really afford it, anyway.

He slumped down beside Snigger and poured another pair of drinks.

'You think he's after me because he believes I killed Rita?'

'Yes – I dunno if he wants to erase you altogether, but I'd say he wants to let his boys rough you up until you weren't fit to walk for a month. That's more his mark … he does it to his non-paying clients – more effective than dragging them to court.'

Jacobs got up from the settee and went to the window. He stared out pensively at the white tower of the University. 'He's the only one who knows about me being involved in drugs?'

'And Ray Silver – and Irish O'Keefe – and me,' he added as an afterthought.

'Silver will keep his trap shut – it pays him to. You're OK and O'Keefe I can't do much about. But it's Draper who's the danger … he sounds cracked enough to cause me real trouble.

Later that evening, Paul slipped as unobtrusively as possible into the Gerrard Street club and made his way straight to the back office. He found the tubby owner adjusting his bowtie before a mirror, in preparation for the announcement of the first cabaret act.

'Can't spare you more than a minute, Golding.'

The Portuguese-Chinese mixture in Silver's blood seemed more than usually prominent tonight, thought Paul. The fat man appeared even more uneasy and twittery than usual.

'I won't spoil your big moment, Ray,' he growled. 'Just give me your order and I'll be off – I don't want to hang around myself, as it happens.'

Silver turned from the mirror and lifted his shoulders in supplication. His sweaty palms were turned to Paul in an age-old gesture of sorrowful regret. 'Sorry, I can't take anything this time.'

'What the hell d'you mean? You always want something!'

'I'm pretty well stocked up … and the bobbies have been a bit too active this last day or two, since your girlfriend got herself killed. I'm laying off for a bit. I don't want to be turned over by the police and have them find drugs on the premises.'

Paul shrugged in annoyance.

'OK … so you don't want anything?'

The Eurasian's eyes took a crafty glint that was not lost on Jacobs. 'Not this time, but I might be wanting a special order soon – quite a big one. May be before you show up again, so can you give me an address or phone number where I can get you, huh?'

Paul ignored the artless attempt to get hold of something to buy off Draper. He went to the door and flung a parting shot over his shoulder.

'I hope you're not going to back out altogether – it costs a packet to organise these trips to the continent and a few duff orders like this knocks all the profit out of it.'

Silver did some more hand spreading. 'Sorry, but I'm playing it nice and safe. Where are you going tomorrow that's costing you all that much?'

'All the way to Munich … a hell of a long train journey just to buy stuff that I may not be able to sell when I get back,' snapped Paul. He cut short the club owner's fawning apologies and stalked away in a bad temper.

Jacobs climbed the stairs to Gerrard Street and went back to his flat. Fifteen minutes after he had left the Nineties Club, Conrad Draper arrived in his flashy limousine and made his way to Silver's office.

Chapter Ten

The Tauern Express leaves Victoria every afternoon at three o'clock, passing through Cologne, Munich and Salzburg, to reach its destination at Klagenfurt. Paul Jacobs climbed aboard twenty minutes before it pulled out, having no idea that Conrad Draper was already sitting in a first class compartment in the next coach.

Snigger had known nothing about this latest move and was unable to warn Paul to be on his guard. He had seen Conrad come into the club late on the previous evening, after Jacobs had left without an order, but had no idea that Ray Silver had passed on the tip that Paul was catching the Munich Express.

Jacobs was travelling under a newly forged passport in the name of Reginald Foster, a post-graduate student from Birmingham University. He did not intend coming back to England in this name for some time. Reginald Foster would go into cold storage in Germany for a few months until he was needed for a return trip. Paul had other plans for making his way back this time.

He settled his luggage on the rack of a second class compartment. He had a rucksack and a small case, in keeping with his role of an elderly but still impoverished research student. Dropping into his reserved seat – he had stretched his student character enough to have a couchette for the night – he pulled out a magazine and relaxed.

He had made all the elaborate preparations for the trip some weeks before. A false passport in the name of Franz Shulman had been mailed out to a hotel in Munich – it would be too embarrassing to be searched by the Customs and have it found on his person. These passports were made for him by an accomplished pen-man in Paddington. They cost him a great deal of money, but he considered that it was good value.

Dead on three o'clock, the long train pulled out on the first stage of its journey to Austria. Both men gazed out from their respective compartments at the wintry London suburbs and then the fields of Kent as the boat-train raced along. Conrad alternatively dozed over his lunchtime whiskies and glanced at the bawdy magazines that he had brought from a Soho shop. Apart from a basal glow of satisfaction about the sweet revenge that was on the way, he had no definite plotting to disturb his lazy mind.

Paul Jacobs' brain, a few yards away, was ticking over at high speed, thinking of details of this trip and the next one, which was a run to Marseilles. In addition, as his eyes roamed over the bleak fields of the Weald, he fretted over Silver's attack of cold feet. This might mean that he would have to reduce his buying or work up new contacts in London if he wanted to keep his profits stable.

As he mulled over his business, Jacobs was oblivious of the man in the next carriage who was determined to kill him.

Gigal had been wrong in thinking that Conrad only wanted to find Paul so that his thugs could give him a beating up. The warped mind of the ex-wrestler had been permanently bruised by the insult he had suffered – when Paul had liquidated Draper's new mistress, he had triggered off the man's latent madness.

Silver's tip-off in the club on the previous night, when Draper had learned of Paul's intention to catch the Saturday train to Munich, had been too great a temptation for him to miss.

He sat in his plush first class compartment, the Webley making a slight bulge in his jacket pocket, without making any effort to make sure that Golding really was on the train. His megalomania assured him that no one would dare interfere with the plans of the great Conrad. He was endowed with blind faith in his own invincibility. Draper would have gone all the way to Bavaria without bothering to confirm that the other man was aboard somewhere, but as it happened, he caught a glimpse of Golding as they were transferring to the cross-channel ferry.

Draper smiled smugly to himself and tapped the automatic in his pocket. He had one great advantage over Golding: he recognised the drug runner at sight from seeing him a few times with Rita, whereas Golding had no reason to know him from Adam.

The bookie had not the slightest idea of how he was going to deal with his enemy when they got to Munich – again his delusions of utter superiority carried him way above such trivial worries. The idea of failure never crossed his mind – the facts that he was alone in a foreign land, without a word of the language and not even a place to stay, only sank in as the train carried him across Europe.

Early the next morning, the big cities of southern Germany rolled past the windows: Karlsruhe, Stuttgart, and Ulm. By the time Augsburg was reached, the last big town before Munich itself, Conrad was forced to think of some plan of action, even if it was only to keep Golding in sight when they reached their destination.

His unimaginative but cunning mind got to work. The more he sat thinking about it, the more difficult his position appeared to be. Though still no thought of failure entered his mind, he began to realise that some careful strategy was needed if he was not to be left standing on the platform whilst Golding vanished in a taxi.

So when the great diesel engine dragged them to a stop at the Hauptbahnhof Munchen, Conrad was already on the step waiting to hop off at the front end. He wanted to intercept Golding before he vanished into the town.

Grasping his suitcase, he stepped off and stood in the

centre of the platform, with the crowds streaming past him. He kept a sharp lookout for his fellow countryman and soon spotted him coming up the platform, his rucksack bowing him slightly.

Conrad began a rather overdone pantomime intended to express the utter bewilderment of an Englishman in a foreign land. He called out in a loud voice to a passing porter.

'Hello, porter! Porter! Oh, for God's sake, doesn't anybody speak English here!'

Several heads, including the porter's, were turned towards him, all quite willing to show their knowledge of that language. Conrad ignored them and stepped across to intercept Golding.

'Sorry to pounce on you, but could you help me?'

Paul Jacobs stopped dead. He had been daydreaming a little, the familiar sounds and sights of his native country having aroused many memories. He stared at the large man standing squarely in his path. A warning bell began ringing faintly in his mind.

'Er, yes ... sure, if I can.'

Where the hell had he seen this chap before? He knew his face but he couldn't place him.

Conrad dropped his case onto the concrete and dragged a small German guidebook from his pocket.

'I knew you were English – heard you talking in the dining car last night, that's why I had the nerve to stop you ... look, I can't speak a bloody word of this lingo and I've got to find somewhere to stay ... can you help me?' .

Paul, cautious and wary now, beat his brains to try to remember where he had seen the man before. Was it at some Customs desk or Immigration office? Was he a narcotics man, or a policeman of some sort? He didn't look it. And that voice ...

'A hotel, you mean – you want me to recommend one?' he stalled, still desperately trying to size Draper up. It was transparently obvious that this encounter was a fake. The whole scene was pure ham. The man was surely too bad a performer to be a detective.

Draper eagerly answered. 'Yes, yes, if you would; I've got to meet a friend on Tuesday – he speaks German – but until he shows up, I'm scuppered!'

'What sort of place did you want?' asked Paul.

Draper eyed the other man warily. Unless he was careful, he would get an address thrust at him and he would lose Golding after all.

'Oh, I don't know. Where do you stay? That should be about my mark,' he ended illogically.

Paul had an answer ready. 'I stay with friends, I'm afraid. But I can recommend a few places, depends on what you want to pay.'

Draper cursed under his breath. For the first time his self-assurance began to wilt. If Golding got away from him now, he might as well get on the train and go home again. He became desperate and his voice shed some of its painfully acquired West End veneer and slid back to Whitechapel.

'Look, chum, couldn't you do me a favour ... come with me in a taxi and drop me off at some hotel? I couldn't even ask for a room in this flaming language.'

There was a sudden clash of cymbals in Paul Jacobs' head. This was the voice on the tape!

Without understanding how the owner came to be standing alongside him, seven hundred miles from London, he accepted the fact and his defence mechanism snapped into action. He must find out more about the man's motives in following him and in this ridiculous farce of pretending not to know him.

'Right, come along this way, we'll get a cab.' He beckoned Conrad and strode in front of him, his mind working furiously. He led the bookie off the platform and out into the wide area in front of the station, where he called a car.

A sleek Mercedes drew up and the driver peered questioningly from the window. Jacobs spoke to him in faultless German. Normally he used language with a painfully acquired foreign accent in keeping with his supposed identity, but in the pressure of events his tongue slipped back into his native speech.

'Take us to Schwabing, go along Leopoldstrasse,' he said. 'I'll tell you exactly where when we get there.'

The cab crawled out into the permanent traffic jam that clogged the Bavarian capital. The two men lounged in the back and exchanged entirely fictitious names and addresses, the bookie professing to be Albert Smith of Croydon, on his way to meet a friend for a winter sporting holiday. Apart from the fact that the snows had not yet come to the Garmisch area, the bookie's racetrack suit, his one small case and lack of skis, cameras, boots, or any of the paraphernalia of winter sports made a complete nonsense of his story.

Just to keep things even, Paul trotted out his Reginald Foster routine about the University. He enquired about Conrad's idea of a hotel.

'Will a pension suit you – you know, a boarding house? I know a place that's very reasonable – clean and cheap.'

Conrad nodded eagerly. He would quite cheerfully have slept in a doss house if it meant keeping Golding in sight.

Paul stared out of the taxi windows at the attractive city. His mind was working at top speed. What the devil was this big moron doing here? Was this more than an attempt at blackmail? Why keep up this stupid pretence of not revealing who he was? Even Jacobs' astute mind failed to guess the real reason for the ex-wrestler's clumsy efforts to follow him halfway across Europe.

Whatever the bookie's motives, they made no difference to the plan that was rapidly forming in Paul's head. This was a heaven-sent opportunity to get rid of Draper well away from the attentions of the British police and must not be passed up.

The self-appointed king of Brewer Street began clumsy efforts to keep tabs on Golding after the taxi ride ended.

'I wonder if we could meet for a drink later on – or I could stand you a meal if you tell me a decent place. Until I find my own way around, I'll be marooned in this damned place.'

Paul agreed readily. He had not the slightest intention of losing sight of Conrad Draper now.

'Sure, I'll call around for you about eight o'clock. I'll show you some of the Munich night life.'

He gave Draper a roguish wink and nudged him with his elbow. This served the double purpose of suggesting a randy night out and also confirmed the suspicion he had about the bulge in Draper's jacket pocket.

The Mercedes had crawled through the city centre and was passing the bombed and fire-torn relics of the Hitler regime, which still stood as a neglected monument near the Odeonsplatz.

Jacobs, almost amused by the patent relief on Draper's face, enlarged on the sights as they passed.

'This is the sort of Montmartre of Munich – the student area – umpteen thousand art students beat the place up every now and then.'

He carried on with a potted guide to the city and Draper nodded dumbly. Apart from trips to the Riviera casinos and the racetracks, like Longchamps, he knew nothing about the continent. Paul gave the driver more instructions and the taxi turned into a side street, the Franz-Josef Strasse. They pulled up at a tall apartment building with the name 'Pension Walther' above the entrance.

Paul jumped out, telling Conrad to wait.

'I'll have to chat up the proprietor a bit, I expect. Rooms are difficult to come by without booking.'

He went inside and found the owner's private room at the back of the ground floor. He knocked and put his head around the door.

The proprietor, a fat crop-headed Rhinelander named Wormser, jumped up in surprise.

'Schrempp! Where the devil did you come from?'

Paul put a finger to his lips. 'Sssh ... none of that Schrempp stuff, he died in forty-four. Look, I want a room for someone. He's outside in a taxi.'

Wormser's piggy eyes stared suspiciously from his fleshy face.

'I'm full up – not a bed in the place.'

'He won't want a bed, Franz ... just a room for the evening. Don't sign him in the register – just give him somewhere to put his case. He won't be back for it, so you're welcome to whatever's in it.'

Wormser's face relaxed and his mouth made an understanding leer. This was something to relieve the tedium of the retirement from violence forced on him by the interest of the War Crimes Commission in Frankfurt.

Draper was soon settled in a room belonging to a patron who was away for a few days. Wormser temporarily removed his belongings and Conrad unsuspectingly arranged his few expensive shirts and socks in the drawers.

Paul Jacobs took the taxi back to his own pension, a few streets away in the Konradstrasse. This was another modest hotel carefully chosen to be in keeping with his supposed identity of a postgraduate student.

He managed to distort his German enough to deceive the manager, then went to his room to think out the timetable for the coming evening. He was still puzzled as to Draper's motive in following him to Germany. It made clear all the byplay in the back office of the Nineties Club the week before, but the basic reason was still obscure.

Paul considered again the possibility that Conrad might

want to kill him, but eventually shrugged it off. He had no idea of the warped fixation in the other man's mind. The gun was difficult to explain, but he assumed that a man with Draper's gangster kink might carry one just for kicks.

He sat staring into space for a long time while pieces of his plan for the disposal of Conrad Draper fell into place.

'If I can't get rid of him with one hand behind my back, I'm losing my grip,' he murmured finally, getting up and stretching himself. 'It should be like stealing a blind man's penny.'

He went out for a meal in the Leopoldstrasse and returned for a quick nap until the afternoon had waned. Around dusk, he made a trip by tram to the warehouse district off Landsberger Strasse, in another part of the city. As in the Brussels episode, he slid into a lonely alleyway and entered an unobtrusive door. A few minutes later he came out with a large brown paper parcel and made his way back to the pension.

About seven o'clock, he went out for a lager and a look at Munich in the early evening. He wandered in the dark down the Leopoldstrasse, crowded with students and the first Sunday evening revellers.

Though it was early December, it had turned suddenly mild. The art students were out in strength, as on a summer evening, sitting on walls with their guitars, shouting and singing to the despair of the Polizei patrolmen. Paintings and sketches were strung on cords between the trees, partly for sale and partly for exhibition. Groups of students crouched around guttering candles stuck in wine bottles, drinking beer and arguing.

Suppressed national pride surged back into Paul's soul as he walked along. This was his Germany, he thought. After all these years posing as a British subject, he still felt this bittersweet feeling when he came back.

Sometimes he regretted the move that had exiled him from Germany for good. Paul had been afraid to return after the first upheavals of peace had subsided. By changing identities with a dead soldier a month before the Luneburg Heath capitulation, he vanished into the chaos of Hamburg and got out on one of the first vessels to use the shattered port. He masqueraded as a seaman and after several more rapid changes of identity, spent a year on a Canadian ship, perfected his already excellent English, then settled in London in forty-seven.

Now as he walked along the candlelit pavements of Munich, this strange man felt a double pride: the pride of still being one of the master race, yet still oddly proud of being a successful British businessman.

The mood passed as he sauntered back to Konradstrasse and by twenty minutes to eight he was ready for the affairs of the night. He took two articles from his case which helped him to merge completely into the Munich scene ... a heavy, black raincoat, tightly belted, and a furry velour trilby. With these on, he looked as if he had been no nearer Piccadilly than Cologne.

He walked round to Franz-Joseph Strasse, appearing every inch a suburban Munchener, and walked in unannounced on Franz Wormser.

'Everything in order?'

'Yes, he's been wandering around – I taught him enough German to go out and ask for a beer this afternoon.' The cropped proprietor paused. 'He's carrying a gun, you know.' He patted his pocket expressively.

Paul Jacobs nodded. 'I felt it in the taxi – that's what I've called to see you about.'

Wormser looked wary. 'I haven't got one to give you, if that's what you're after. I'm not sticking my neck out that far.'

Paul shook his head.

'I don't want a gun, but I want something to sap him with – something nice and small.'

Wormser grinned. This was more to his liking. He took

a bunch of keys from his pocket and went over to a steel cupboard against the wall of the shabby room, which was office and bedroom combined. He opened the bottom half and took out a wooden box.

'Help yourself,' he offered, putting the box on a table.

Paul looked inside and saw a collection of knives, blackjacks, and even a pair of brass knuckledusters.

Paul weighed a couple of coshes in his hands and settled on a short sap made of hard black rubber.

'I'll take this – I don't want to kill him. Just send him to sleep.'

Wormser looked disappointed. 'No killing?'

Paul looked coolly at him. 'Later! Just like the old days, eh, Sergeant … remember Krefeld?'

He walked out without another word, leaving a suddenly pale Wormser behind him, a Wormser who had taken note of the fact that his freedom, if not his life, depended on Schrempp's mouth staying closed.

Paul climbed the stairs to Draper's room, the blackjack deep in his raincoat pocket.

'Ready?'

'Yeah – let's go.'

Draper's speech was an incongruous mixture of Mayfair, Bowery, and Whitechapel. When he let his grip slide on the first, it was the one from beyond Aldgate pump that popped up – the one that Paul Jacobs had pinned down from his recollections of the voice on the tape.

They took another taxi back to the centre of the city. Each sat chatting with false sincerity, each with a weapon in his pocket and murder in his heart. The car dropped them at the Karsplatz, the focal point of Munich, a confused tangle of traffic lights, tramlines and signalling policemen.

True to his word, Conrad stood Jacobs an excellent meal at a nearby restaurant. They wined and dined in a huge first-floor sunroom, looking down on the kaleidoscope of moving lights below. As with Rita, Paul felt no twinge of conscience as he made small talk across the table. Again, like the Rita affair, he did his best to get the bookie to drink as heavily as possible, without taking too much himself. Getting Conrad to swallow alcohol was easy, but the big man had a head like a rhinoceros.

'What now, then?' asked Conrad, wiping his mouth with a napkin after five courses and three rounds of spirits.

'Let's see something of the back streets,' suggested Jacobs. He slipped his hand into his pocket as he put his raincoat on and felt the smooth rubber cosh lying ready for action. Innocent to the touch, it could be a deadly weapon in the right hands.

They walked out into the late evening crowds and dodged among the tramcars to enter the warren of small streets in the old town. They wandered for a time, in and out of bars, Paul still forcing the other to drink as fast as he was able. As they went further from the main shopping streets, dozens of bars and night clubs spilled light and music onto the pavements. Drunks and kissing couples shrank into doorways as they passed, taking them for patrolling Polizei in the gloom.

Draper seemed fascinated by the place – the counterpart of his own Soho. He almost forgot his purpose in being there. He certainly failed to wonder how Golding knew his way about so well. They went from bar to bar in quick succession, Paul drinking about a third of the bookie's intake of spirits and pilsener.

Around eleven o'clock, they dived into a striptease joint on the Platzl, opposite the centuries-old brewery, the Hofbrauhaus. Again Draper seemed absorbed in the show, which they saw from the bar at the rear of the hall. Draper drank everything that was put in front of him and the dope runner began to get impatient.

'Come on, you must see the Hofbrauhaus – it's just

over there.'

He dragged the reluctant Conrad across the narrow road and they plunged into the most famous of the Munich beer gardens. It was now more of a tourist attraction than a genuine drinking house, but at that time of the year there were few visitors and most of the customers were hard-drinking locals. The central courtyard was deserted. In the summer, a band played here amid tables in the open air. In the bare tap-rooms there was plenty of life.

Again Draper sat enthralled. An oom-pah-pah band thumped away in the corner and a buxom maid brought them a pair of litre mugs of draught beer. The flagged floor was swimming with slopped drink and the whole place smelt of hundreds of years of carousing.

Conrad's murderous plans vaporised for the moment while he absorbed the atmosphere. He had devoted little time to plotting in any case. So far he had thought of nothing but a sudden show of brute strength in some dark lane on the way home. With his wrestler's experience, he reckoned he could snap Golding's neck in two seconds flat Then he would drop him in an alley, go home, and catch the first train back to Calais in the morning.

Like Jacobs, he thought the fact that they were so far from the Metropolitan Police was an opportunity not to be missed. The gun was a second line attack in case anything went wrong with the first plan. For the moment he was content to drink pilsener from the huge earthenware stein and chew radishes, which seemed to be the traditional fare of the Hofbrauhaus.

After a few minutes, Jacobs rose abruptly.

'What about a Jimmy Riddle?' he demanded. 'You've been drinking all night – it's about time for one.'

Conrad rose amiably and followed him out into the cobbled courtyard. The metal tables and chairs stood dismal and deserted as they made their way across to a battered door blatantly labelled *Pissoir*.

Paul pushed it open and let Conrad go in first. In the grim and odorous dungeon that served as the gentlemen's toilet, there were two men about to leave.

The open doors of the cubicles showed that no one else was there, so Jacobs seized his chance the second the door closed behind the two men.

Draper was at the wall fumbling with his clothes when Paul stepped back slightly, slid the cosh smoothly from his pocket and brought it down viciously on the back of the man's neck. He had lost none of his wartime expertise and, as the black rubber struck the junction of head and neck, Draper began to fall, already unconscious.

Only four or five seconds had gone by since the door had swung shut on the last customers. Now it burst open again and three roistering herrenvolk barged into the lavatory. Conrad had not yet reached the ground and Jacobs, whipping the sap back into his pocket, grabbed at his waist and stopped him from slumping right to the floor.

'Give us a hand, boys!' he called in his best local accent. 'He can't hold his drink, the fool – thought he came in to be sick but he's passed out on me.'

The slightly tipsy young men good-naturedly helped him to drag the comatose Draper outside and dump him on a chair in the courtyard.

'He does this every time, always spoils the evening,' grumbled Paul, 'now I suppose I'll have to get the bastard home to his wife.'

One of the men helped him to drag the heavy body to the arch which led out into the street. The other patrons and the serving women hardly gave them a glance. Paralytic customers had been commonplace in the Hofbrauhaus for many centuries and the sight of another being helped home by his friends was no novelty.

Paul waved to a taxi which was just unloading at the strip joint opposite. As he waited, a black uniformed policeman strolled past, a revolver belted over his long greatcoat. He looked idly at the two men supporting the 'drunk', but as there seemed to be no disturbance he passed them by.

The Opel drove across the road and with an effort Paul and his genial helper managed to stuff the sixteen stone of dead weight into the back of the car. Paul followed it and leaned forward to the driver.

'Take us to the Brudermühlbrücke, please. You know, down in Thalkirchen.'

The taxi man let in his clutch, but threw a surprised glance over his shoulder.

'Brudermühl bridge! This time of night? But the zoo is closed, heh!' He guffawed at his joke.

The area Jacobs had mentioned was a large tract of parkland on the banks of the River Isar. It was about two miles out of the city centre, in the southern suburbs. There were playing fields, a famous zoo, and natural woodland, but it seemed an unlikely place for a pair of drunks on a Sunday night.

Paul leant further forward over the seat, giving a fine performance of inebriated intimacy.

'See, I've got to sober this fool up before he gets home. His wife will kill him – and me – if he gets home dead drunk again tonight. He lives just over the bridge, in Geising; so if I can sit him in the fresh air for half an hour, then make him walk, he'll come round – he always does.'

The driver nodded understanding and sped off down the river embankment towards Thalkirchen. It was now well gone midnight and though the city centre was still lively, the residential areas were deserted. Apart from a few hurrying cars, there was little traffic along the Wittelsbacherstrasse and Paul could see that the journey was only going to take a few minutes.

He had judged the blow he had given to Draper so that he should stay unconscious for twenty minutes to half-an-hour.

The Opel sped along the river road, the Isar glinting in the moonlight on their left. They turned off amongst the trees and took a short cut to the Brudermühlbrücke, which formed one of the main river crossings in the south part of the city.

The driver looked incredulous when Paul told him to pull up alongside a park bench just on the town side of the bridge.

'You must be crazy to get him out here,' he protested. 'Geising is nearly a kilometre from here!'

Paul ignored him and began lugging the limp form of Draper from the car towards the seat. The driver grudgingly helped him to lift the big man's feet up so that Conrad lay flat on the wooden slats.'

Paul followed the cabbie back to the car, deliberately weaving as he went.

'S'all right, driver – he'll be sick in a minute, then he'll wake up and be as bright as a new mark. I've seen it all too often, I don't know why I keep doing it for him.'

He stuffed some notes into the man's hand, giving him a generous tip. The car, with a last questioning look from the cabby, slid away and Paul stood until its tail lights had vanished down the long ramp of the bridge.

He looked anxiously up and down the road. It was clear for the moment, so he darted back to the bench, dragged Draper off with a thump onto the ground and began rolling him towards the grass bank behind the seat.

Here the ground fell away sharply, having been built up about twenty feet to make the approach ramp to the bridge. There was a neat border of flowers and bushes at the edge of the steep slope, and right at the bottom a flat grassy area bordering on the edge of the river. As he got Draper's inert body as far as the flowers, a sudden glare of headlights lit up the road behind him.

Like a flash he dropped to the ground behind the seat and watched a black police BMW flash past, its blue light

118

revolving on the roof as it raced to some emergency call. Even though Paul knew it could have no connection with him, the sight of it so soon after his attack on Draper made him nervous and less cautious than he should have been.

As soon as the patrol car passed, he went back to the bookie and bent over him to give him the final push over the edge of the bank. As he did so, he collected a violent kick in the stomach which made him vomit instantly and stagger back to fall in agony on the ground.

If Draper had been fit at that moment it would have been all over for Paul in a matter of seconds, as he was paralysed with pain. But Conrad had spent his energy in that one kick, and was still semi-conscious. He grunted and squirmed about trying to scrabble himself on to his knees. His head was a ball of agony from the blow in the Hofbrauhaus and he could hardly see for the watering of his eyes and the dizziness in his brain.

For a full half minute the two men gasped and groped like two blind lunatics, unable to speak or get to their feet.

Paul Jacobs began to recover first, spurred on by the wavering memory of the gun in the other man's pocket. He hauled himself to a sitting position and fought down the waves of nausea from his bruised stomach. Desperately trying to hold on to consciousness, he saw that Conrad was trying to climb to his feet. He seemed in as much distress as Jacobs, grovelling along the ground, rubbing his head and eyes with one hand. As Paul cleared the fog in his head and began to take some proper breaths, he saw Draper reach a crouching position and fumble in his pocket for the pistol.

With a tremendous spurt, Paul pulled himself up, staggered forwards and kicked Draper full in the face. He fell back with the effort and ended up squatting on the ground facing Conrad, both of them slumped in the earth of the ornamental border.

In spite of the blow in the face, the bookie had got his

automatic free and was pointing it waveringly at Jacobs, now only six feet away – even a battered hulk like Draper could hardly miss at that range.

Conrad mumbled through bruised lips. 'I'm going to kill you, Golding.'

Chapter Eleven

It was a week after the exhumation before Benbow had any glimmer of a breakthrough on the Rita Laskey case.

He and Bray were lunching in the basement canteen at Scotland Yard. Over apple tart and coffee, the Admiral let drop a few ripe remarks on the reluctance of the residents of Soho to give him any help.

'Bleeding lot of yobs,' he crackled, stirring away angrily with his plastic spoon, 'Once you get north of Coventry Street, you need thumbscrews to get them to give you so much as their ruddy name.'

Turnbull was sitting with them, calm and serene as ever.

'What have you got so far, Archie?'

'Very little,' grunted Benbow. 'We've got the name of this boyfriend of Laskey's from a garage chap a few streets away. He was called Golding and had a new Mark X Jag.'

Can't you trace him through that?' asked the laboratory officer.

Benbow shook his head. 'Cunning so-and-so had registered it in the name of Paul Golding of the Newman Street address – insurance and all. We found it had been sold at a St. Alban's car auction two days after the murder – again under a false name and address.'

'That surely marks him down as the guilty party,' chipped in Bray, who had said this to Benbow at least three times already.

'No, it doesn't – it bloody well doesn't!' answered the chief inspector heatedly. 'You try saying that in court and you'll have defence counsel riding you like a donkey! He could have covered up his tracks like this just to protect his affair with the girl from getting back to his wife.'

'Anything else?' prompted Turnbull.

'Damn all, this Golding has vanished off the face of the earth ... though for all I know he might be sitting at the next table.'

He scowled around the crowded canteen as if he hoped to catch the elusive Golding red-handed with egg and chips.

'He's just a name ... a lousy false name,' he muttered then glugged down his coffee.

Turnbull began chipping away at his pipe bowl with some strange instrument. 'So you're up against it? Nothing in the flat?'

Benbow shook his head.

'Clean as a whistle. We've been over it a couple of times. Your boys have had dust and God knows what from there, but the answer's a lemon.'

'What are you going to do about it?'

Benbow's bright eyes flashed. 'Work, boy – work! I reckon we haven't heard the last of this fellow Golding. Something will crop up. And we've got four other jobs on the go. Our office looks like a wastepaper depot. This Golding lark will have to take a back seat until something breaks. I've sent the ACC my report on it this morning – if he doesn't like it, he can stuff it!' he ended pugnaciously.

As if to give his pessimism the lie, things began to happen during the next twenty-four hours. Soon after lunch, when he had started to attack the mountain of paperwork in his office, one of the Drug Squad sergeants rang through.

'Roberts here, sir ... may be nothing in it, but we picked up a chap over the weekend who might be of interest to you. He's charged with unlawful possession ... a dozen decks of heroin on him. He's in a bad way, been on the hard stuff for a long time. Remanded for a week, in

Brixton but he's starting to twitch already.'

Benbow conjured up a nauseating picture of the man in the hell of a drugless existence in prison. He frowned.

'OK, but how's that going to help me?'

'You sent Bray over the other day to ask if we had any angles on the injection marks on that Laskey woman. He mentioned that one of her calling places was the Nineties Club. We've never had a squeak about that place till now – as far as peddling goes – but this junkie we picked up in Leicester Square has started to talk … and he mentioned that place.'

Benbow began to see the light.

'Ah, this sounds more like it. We've been up a gum tree with this one, about time we had a lead from somewhere. Is he ready to blow the gaff?'

'I think so. The doc here says that he'll have to give him a bit of the dope to keep him sane but I think he'll hold off long enough for us to work on him – within Judge's Rules, of course.'

Benbow ignored the sarcasm in Roberts' voice.

'When can we see this bird?' he asked.

'This afternoon would be best. He'll go off the boil once he gets a shot from the M.O.'

Later that afternoon, Benbow and Bray stepped through the barred inner gate of Brixton Prison into the bleak courtyard. There were formal flower beds set out in grim regularity but nothing could detract from the harsh surroundings of the ugly building. Men in drab overalls slouched around with brooms and buckets and trusties moved around with something approaching jauntiness in their step, their armbands worn with the pride of the V.C.

A warder led them to the remand block. After a ritual of opening and closing knobless doors, they found the man they wanted shut up in a small room with the sergeant from the Drug Squad.

Bray had not seen an addict in the withdrawal state

before and he came away from Brixton with no desire to see another. The man, an emaciated skeleton with septic sores on his face, sat shaking on a chair in the middle of the small room in which he was being interviewed. His eyes were staring and his jaw chattered so much that he could hardly answer. A coarse prison blanket was draped around his shoulders but he seemed to rattle with cold, in spite of the oppressive central heating.

Sergeant Roberts straightened up when they came in and gave them a summary of his results so far.

'Our friend here, name of Jack Feiner, sir – he's being very sensible. The doctor will be along soon – if he helps us all he can, I think we can recommend that he gets some medical attention.'

He winked at Benbow and the haggard wreck, now two days without an injection, raised a gaunt face in supplication. Bray felt sick.

'Better come outside, Roberts,' suggested Benbow.

They went into the corridor and Bray shut the door. A warder was left standing impassively over the pathetic figure.

'What's he said?' asked the Admiral.

'Told us about two people who are flogging decks of heroin. One is a barrow boy we've had our eye on for some time. The other is Ray Silver, the owner of the Nineties Club.'

Benbow considered this. 'Doesn't get us any further on the Golding angle. Let's have another word with him.'

They went back into the room and Benbow stood over the trembling figure in the chair.

'You used to get your heroin from Ray Silver, that right?'

The man stuttered something and nodded his head.

'When was the last time?'

Feiner murmured something unintelligible and the chief inspector lowered his head to listen. He eventually gathered that the man never dealt directly with Silver, but knew that his waiter did the distributing.

'But do you definitely say that Ray Silver is behind it?' persisted Benbow.

Feiner's head trembled on his emaciated shoulders. 'No, I only think so,' he mumbled. 'I only worked with Albert, the waiter'

He had been going to the Nineties until a month before. He maintained, as firmly as he was able, that he had never heard of anyone called Rita Laskey or Paul Golding. Benbow spent a few more minutes snapping questions, bending low over the man to speak sharply into his ear and try to pick up the garbled replies from the pathetic remnant of what once had been a man.

Feiner explained that he got the drugs from the waiter in an envelope which was put under the bill when the man brought it for drinks purchased in the club. Feiner would put the money for it on the tray and get only nominal change for the sake of appearances.

He had no proof, direct proof, much to Benbow's chagrin. Roberts was even more annoyed, as he was more directly concerned in the drug trade. Feiner could not say that Silver was in on the racket and it was only his word that Albert was dealing in heroin. The evidence would not be good enough to take to court unless they could get some corroboration from another witness or find drugs on the premises.

'We've got enough to get a warrant for this club, though,' said Benbow. 'We'd better make arrangements to turn it over pretty soon.'

The addict's mind began to wander after a time and his wits seemed shattered. The detectives left the cell and walked back to the great steel grid that closed the inner side of the entrance arch.

'I'm sure he's speaking the truth,' said Roberts seriously. 'Under all that shaking, he's still ticking over mentally. I've seen 'em ten times worse than that and they get better in a week – until they get their hands on the next lot of junk.'

They were checked out of the prison and continued their talk on the way back to the Yard in the car.

'We can't really expect any tie-up between this chap and the Laskey affair,' said Benbow. 'The only link is drugs and that's getting so common around the town these days that it needn't be a common denominator at all ... so go ahead and knock off this Silver character if you can, we'll come along for the laughs if you don't mind ... we're due for a bloody miracle and we may pick up something useful.'

Roberts looked worried. 'We can't touch Silver unless he's got dope on his premises. I think I could risk knocking off this waiter but, if he doesn't admit anything and we don't get any confirmation, I'll never get a charge to stick.'

At seven o'clock that night, armed with a search warrant, they arrived in Gerrard Street. Benbow, Bray, and Roberts, together with a detective constable and two uniformed PCs, pushed past the doorman with a brief flourish of the warrant and descended into the club.

At that early hour, there were only a couple of hard drinking types at the bar. The band had not yet arrived and all the tables were empty. The detectives, looking more like Yard men than anything television had ever dreamed up, marched past Snigger on their way to the office. If they hoped to catch Silver red-handed with a sack of morphine over his shoulder, they were out of luck. He was sitting behind his desk, fast asleep.

He woke with a start and stared owlishly at the intruders. For a moment he thought it was a return of Conrad's hooligans and fear leapt into his eyes.

'Who the devil are you?'

'Police officers – are you Ray Silver?' asked Roberts brusquely.

Silver paled slightly but kept his face well under control.

'That's me. What d'you want?'

'We have reason to suspect that you may be in unlawful possession of narcotics in contravention of the Dangerous Drugs Act … in other words, chum, we want to see if you've got any stuff stacked away here.'

Bray, watching Silver's face, could have sworn that he saw relief cross it. He seemed to become unconcerned, almost bouncy, waving his hand around the room.

'You must be off your chump, boy – but help yourself. I suppose you've got a warrant.'

'Here it is.' Roberts half-pulled a form from his pocket but made no attempt to show it to Silver.

'Carry on, then … what bum has been trying to make trouble for me?'

Benbow ignored him.

'Where's your waiter?'

For the first time, the Eurasian looked uneasy.

'I don't know – he should be there. Why ask?'

'He's taken a powder by the look of it,' snapped Benbow, 'but he'll have some awkward questions to face when we pick him up.'

It took a week to find Albert, as it turned out. Getting a tip-off on the internal phone from the doorman, the waiter had nipped smartly up the rear fire escape and gone to earth in Stepney, until a disgruntled junkie had shopped him to the local police.

Back in the club, the Admiral had another poser for Ray Silver.

'Ever heard of Jack Feiner?' he rapped.

Silver had never heard the name, although he would probably have recognised the addict's face. He was able to put on a genuinely puzzled expression and shake his head with convincing innocence.

Benbow sighed. 'Come on then, Roberts, let's have a look around – give me your keys, Silver.'

The proprietor handed them over and sat complacently as the policemen rooted through all his drawers and cupboards. Bray and a PC pulled up the carpets and looked for loose floorboards, they sounded the walls and moved the pictures – all without finding anything incriminating.

'The big key is the one for the safe,' sneered Silver with offensive helpfulness.

Benbow felt from the start that they would find nothing in the office and cursed silently. The big safe held a few hundred pounds in cash, some ledgers, stock books, and an empty steel drawer. There was nothing else to be seen in it.

Benbow was turning away in disgust when he caught a wink from the Drug Squad man. Roberts made a gesture with his thumb that clearly meant that he wanted Silver out of the room.

'Nothing here, Bray,' said Benbow loudly. 'Take Mr Silver out into the other rooms here and ask him to open all the cupboards for you, and try to find that bloody waiter.'

He threw the bunch of keys over and Bray shepherded the grinning owner outside. When the door had closed, Benbow dropped to his knees beside Roberts who was still staring into the safe.

'What's all the mystery?'

'Look – in the crack where those runners for the drawer are fixed.'

The sergeant pointed to a pair of supports which were welded on to the sides of the safe to support the drawer. Benbow craned his thick neck nearer.

'Ah, that white stuff, you mean – in the cracks?'

'Yeah, might be nothing but if it's dope we've got something to throw at him – he's so damn cocky that he's obviously unloaded all his stock. He must have got a whisper somehow.'

As he spoke, Roberts was carefully brushing the few grains of white powder from the runners into a clean envelope that he took from the desk. There were a few more on the opposite side and he added these to the collection.

'No need to put that greasy swine on his guard if it is morphine or heroin. And if it isn't, it'll save us from looking damn fools.'

They went to the bar and with the help of the detective constables, shifted all the bottles, pulled down the glasses, and explored the cupboards below the great engraved mirrors.

Snigger looked on uneasily and almost blew a blood vessel when he saw one of the men push aside his pile of carefully prepared cigarette packets in order to tap the back walls of a cupboard. For a moment, he thought that the detective was going to look through the cartons themselves but, at the last minute, he collected them up and replaced them. Snigger let his breath out in a long controlled sigh of sheer relief, but he was soon disturbed again by Benbow summoning him to the office.

Leaving Molly to look after the disarranged bar, and the two already inebriated patrons, he followed Silver and the policeman back to the room at the rear of the club. Here Benbow and Roberts put them through a snappy interrogation.

Where was Albert? Did they admit to any dealing in drugs? Did they know of any addicts amongst the customers? A string of accusative questions fell like water on so many ducks' backs. Snigger maintained a shocked indignant pose, while Silver blandly denied knowledge of anything at all.

Eventually, Benbow gave up and led the procession back to the front door. The Eurasian pranced behind, still sweating slightly but as cocky as a fat bantam.

'Barking up the wrong tree, Inspector. Your snout must have been having you on ... you ought to know I run a respectable business.'

He watched them drive off, blissfully unaware of the few grains of dusty powder carefully tucked away in Sergeant Roberts' breast pocket.

Chapter Twelve

A grey, cloudy dawn was breaking when Gunther Frey set out with his poodle on their regular morning walk.

Gunther worked in an office in the centre of Munich and it was an act of faith with him to take Mitzi out before she was left alone in the flat all day. Every morning, they left the door in Morassistrasse and walked along the embankment to the Ludwigsbrücke, where they crossed the Isar.

It was cold and wet underfoot, the weather having changed from the mildness of the previous evening. Mitzi pranced along at the end of her red lead, while Gunther, still half-asleep, trudged behind with his head buried in the upturned collar of his overcoat. The street lights were still on as the pair crossed the bridge.

They walked along the path that split the river lengthwise, across the top of a breakwater that joined up two islands in the river. Behind, on one island, lay the great bulk of the Deutschsmuseum. Ahead, the flood weir carried on to the next island which carried the Maximilianbrücke. The grey waters swirled sullenly alongside Gunther as he stopped to unhook the little dog's lead.

Mitzi shot off, pirouetting and prancing on the deserted path. The grey sky and the sodium lamps shone on the water as Gunther tramped on, thinking about his income tax. The surroundings were too familiar for him to spare them a glance. Then Mitzi darted away and began to yap incessantly.

She had stopped at a railing on the deep side of the weir

and here, wagging her trim little tail, she kept up a persistent staccato yapping.

'Ach, be quiet, for Heaven's sake,' muttered her master, walking past. Mitzi stayed put and Gunther had to come back to her. 'Right, back on your lead then,' he threatened, as she continued to stare down and bark at the river.

As he stooped to fix her lead to the collar, he casually followed her intent gaze down into the swirling waters. Bobbing sluggishly in a blind angle of the concrete buttresses, were the shoulders of a man.

Every few seconds, eddies in the water would roll the body slightly so that the back of the head and buttocks appeared. The second time this happened, Gunther's horrified eyes saw a jagged wound at the back of the lower ribs, as if something had burst out from inside, bloodied flesh gaping from a long tear in the jacket.

He took a grip on himself and looked to see if the river was likely to dislodge the corpse from the backwater and carry it over the weir. It seemed to be making no progress downstream, however, and taking a chance on its not getting swept away in his absence, Gunther Frey began running with Mitzi back to the Ludwigsbrücke and the nearest telephone.

'One bullet is still in there, lodged in the spine.' The pathologist announced this blandly to the court judge, who, to his sorrow, had to be present at all criminal post-mortem examinations in Munich.

Two mortuary attendants lifted the big body from the X-ray machine in the comer, to the stainless-steel operating table in the middle of the room. The scene was the basement chamber that was the forensic mortuary of the Munich medical college, not far from the part of the river where the body had so recently been found.

The judge sat uncomfortably on a hard chair at the side

of the bare white-tiled chamber. 'What about that wound in the back?' he asked.

'Pah! A red herring – nothing to do with the death.' The pathologist, Korb, was a small hard-faced man with sparse red hair.

'One bullet entered the front of the chest and didn't come out again. The other went in the throat and straight out of the side of the neck.' He waved a rubber-covered hand at the corpse as the attendants settled it on the table. 'That gash must have happened as the body was floating down river, probably caught against a tree stump or a bridge support.'

He turned back to the body and, knife in hand, stood impatiently while the assistants fussed around getting things ready. A police inspector and a uniformed patrolman stood by as Korb began his examination.

The elderly judge slumped in his seat with a sigh. He had seen too many post-mortems, but they still revolted him. He envied the British system, where the only contact the judiciary has with blood and gore was through the hygienic medium of foolscap documents.

Korb was looking intently at the exterior of the body again, before starting to cut. The clothing had already been carefully removed and lay on a side table, each garment labelled and packed in a plastic bag.

The pathologist studied the face, neck, and stomach, then an attendant rolled it over for him to see the back. Eventually he came back to the neck again.

'Shot twice from the front. Probably the first shot was in the neck. It could hardly have been fatal – it passed through the windpipe but missed all the important arteries – too far forwards.'

'Why was it the first shot, Herr Doctor?' asked the police inspector respectfully. Korb was one always to be used with respect. His acid tongue and temper were renowned in Bavarian police circles.

'Because the wound in the chest must have penetrated the heart and caused almost immediate death,' snapped Korb. 'One would hardly shoot a mortally wounded man a second time in such a trivial manner.'

The inspector had reservations about a shot through the windpipe being trivial, but he kept his mouth shut.

'What sort of range was he shot from, doctor?' asked the judge.

The pathologist thumbed at the spread out clothing and then pointed at the neck of the corpse.

'Not much help from the suit after being stirred around in the Isar for hours, but the skin here tells us a thing or two.'

The judge rose and walked over to the post-mortem table. He saw a neat hole punched in the throat at the front, with a faint speckling of black on the surrounding skin.

'This one was pretty close, but not contact,' explained Korb, 'The entrance hole is not jagged from the tearing effect of the cartridge gases as it would be at a mere few centimetres range, but it was near enough to produce this tattooing from flecks of un-burnt powder on the surrounding flesh.'

'So what sort of distance, sir?' sought the inspector, pencil and notebook hovering at the ready.

Korb made a gesture of impatience.

'Can't be exact, man. The type of weapon, the size of the propellant, the age of the cartridge, the type of powder – they all make a difference. These new explosives produce very little powder burning, not like the old black stuff.' He seemed to savour some past memory for a moment then hurried on with the work.

'Say less than half a metre – probably quite a bit less.'

He bent very near the dead man's neck and examined it minutely.

'No singeing of the hairs on his neck – again probably more than a dozen or so centimetres, but less than fifty …

does it matter?' he ended with annoyance.

'We try to reconstruct these affairs, doctor,' said the judge mildly. 'So far the inspector here tells me that the site of the killing is known. A gardener in Thalkirchen reported vandalism to the police early this morning. There were signs of a disturbance in a flower bed on the Brudermühlbrücke, and at the bottom of the slope at the river's edge, there were bloodstains and signs of dragging of a body into the water. That right, inspector?'

The judge, sorry for the detective's brow-beating at the hands of Korb, was sheltering him under his wing with kind words.

'Yes, judge, a regular fight must have gone on from the edge of the road right down the bank to the water. I've got a skin-diver searching the river bed now, looking for the weapon – it may have been thrown in after the corpse.'

'Some hope!' muttered the pathologist crossly.

'What size gun would you think it will be?' asked the indefatigable policeman.

'Small hole – hard to tell, really. Something less than nine-millimetre, I should say – not a Luger anyway.'

He pointed to the X-ray, still dripping developer, which hung on an illuminated box on the wall. 'Have a look at that, the bullet is buried in the eighth dorsal vertebra in the middle of the back. You can get some idea of the calibre from that, but I'll be getting it out for you soon, anyway.'

After looking at a similar hole in the chest, the doctor began the bloody business of the internal examination. The judge noted that he was particularly interested in the teeth.

'The fillings seem a bit odd-looking ... can't place what it is, but I don't pretend to be a forensic odontologist; I'll get a colleague down to look at them. They certainly aren't local work.'

The examination went on for half an hour, being punctuated by scarifying flashes from the photographic flashguns fixed in the ceiling over the table.

The judge sat patiently, his thoughts gently on his disturbed breakfast – it was still only ten o'clock, the police had moved fast after Gunther had reported the body in the river. The detective scribbled in his notebook whenever Dr Korb muttered some scrap of information, and the patrol man stood immobile the whole time, chewing the cud like some sturdy bullock.

Eventually the pathologist threw down his knife with a clang and went to a sink to rinse the blood from his gloves. The judge slowly came back to earth and the eager inspector stood almost panting for the final revelations.

'Shot through the chest almost dead centre,' began Korb, pushing off the tap with an elbow. 'The second entrance wound is just to the left of the centre of the breastbone, quite low down. So it's gone straight through the heart and finished up in the spine. Here it is, Inspector, if you want it for the lab.'

He walked back to the post-mortem table and carefully picked up a shining bullet with a rubber-tipped forceps, so as not to harm any identifying marks.

'You're lucky it's not deformed, even though it has gone through two bits of bone ... odd calibre, looks something like a six-millimetre.'

The detective took a small cardboard box from his pocket and laid the bullet reverently in a bed of cotton wool. 'Yes, doctor, I doubt if it came from a German pistol. It's copper-jacketed, so it's from an automatic, not a revolver, in all probability.'

He gave it to the waiting uniformed man, with instructions to rush it to the ballistics laboratory of the police department.

'Ask them if they can identify the make of weapon as soon as possible, tell them we've got no gun to compare it with at present.'

The black-uniformed patrolman saluted briskly, coming to life at last. After he had hurried out, Korb spoke again.

'Anyone missing from the city lately?'

'No, sir … we've had a few girls and a couple of children reported this week, but no man for a fortnight – and the last few of those were nothing like him.' The detective gestured to the opened body on the slab.

The pathologist smiled cynically. 'Don't worry about the fortnight; this chap's only been dead a short time. When I saw him first at nine o'clock, his temperature was still thirty degrees centigrade. Even in the Isar in winter he couldn't have been dead longer than say, twelve hours.'

The judge bobbed his head wisely.

'Are we going to get any help from you in identifying him?'

'General stuff only at present,' replied Korb, drying his hands on a cloth while he gazed thoughtfully at the remains. 'Approximate age from appearances and X-rays of some bones. He appears to be in his middle thirties. Then height, weight – all that stuff is written on the form there. No scars or tattoos to be seen.'

He reached for an open jar of stomach contents and put it to his nose. He offered it to the judge but the older man jerked his head back. 'Just tell me, doctor – I'll take your word for it,' he said wryly.

'Drink – a strong smell of beer and spirits. I wonder where he was last night. He certainly took a skinful.' He took another sniff at the jar, all revulsion having left him years before.

'Another thing, judge, he has small injection marks on his arms which are septic in some places – looks exactly like the unsterile jabs that a drug addict gives himself. I'll get an analysis done, but that will take a day or two.'

'He's a big man, doctor,' ventured the inspector.

'Yes, heavily muscled. He has some thickening of the eyebrows and a twisted nose which might suggest that he was used to being in a fight now and then. I've seen it in many strong-arm criminals, not necessarily boxers.'

'You say his fillings look foreign – what about his clothes, any lead there?' asked the judge.

'All the pockets emptied and the labels torn out, sir,' explained the inspector. 'Good quality suit, I just don't know whether it's foreign manufacture or not. All Western clothes look much the same, except to an expert tailor. The torn labels were almost certainly done by the killer at the time of death, the rips are fresh and deliberately confined to the inner pockets and neckbands of the shirt and vest.'

The judge got up and went to look at the clothing.

'So to add up all we know, doctor, we've got a big man of possibly foreign origin, who has been shot twice, the one through the chest having killed him. He was either drunk or had been drinking heavily, and he may have been taking small quantities of narcotics – right?'

Korb nodded abruptly. 'You can add that the first shot through the neck was a wild one, at close range and the second one a more deliberate discharge, possibly at a slightly greater distance, designed to kill. From the signs of the struggle on the bridge, with absence of blood at the top of the slope, it seems that they fought up there, but did not use the weapon until they reached the bottom.'

The detective took up the tale here. 'The killer must have been cool enough to empty the dead man's pockets, rip out the tabs, and then push him into the river ... I wish I knew what he did with the gun.'

By the afternoon a fairly firm opinion as to the deceased's country of origin was arrived at by the dental expert, who declared that the technique and materials of the numerous tooth fillings were typically British.

The detective was a little sceptical about relying too much on this evidence, but he had dramatic confirmation from two directions within the next few hours. Firstly, the ballistics department reported on the bullet extracted from the dead man's spinal column. The inspector muttered a summary of it to his assistant.

'Not a metric size projectile ... a .25 inch copper-clad bullet, corresponding to 6.35 millimetres ... from the rifling pattern left by the barrel it must have been fired from an automatic weapon with six right-hand grooves with a pitch of one turn in twenty-five centimetres. The groove width was 0.56 mm and the land width 2.65 mm ... this corresponds to the specifications of the British Webley self-loading pistol, made in two models, one hammerless, both of .25 inch calibre. One has a short free-standing barrel, is small and is unlike any other German or Continental weapon.'

Almost before he had digested all this, a motorcycle roared up to headquarters with a courier sent from the Brudermühlbrücke with a pistol that an aqualung diver had just grovelled from the bed of the Isar.

It was a .25 Webley automatic.

Already a photograph of the dead man, touched up to look as lifelike as possible, had been printed and, armed with a copy, a squad of police were questioning airport staff, railwaymen, and taxi drivers.

At seven thirty, a cab driver who had not seen the photograph but had heard of the location of the murder, came forward to say that he had taken two men to the bridge around midnight.

While he was in the C.I.D. being questioned, a detective brought in another taxi man who recognised the dead person as a fare he had taken from the railway station to the Pension Walther.

The detective inspector soon found that both drivers agreed that the dead man's companion on both trips must have been the same fellow. The only point of dispute was that the first taxi man said that the man spoke good German with a Cologne accent, while the one who took the pair to Thalkirchen swore that the second man was Munich born and bred.

The time of the train that they had left was checked and was found to be the Tauern Express from Ostend. A call was made to Interpol in Lyon for assistance, asking for the names of all male passengers who had booked on that journey to Munich.

The inspector spent part of the night looking for the second man, who was now the prime suspect. The description from the cab drivers was too vague to be of any use – Golding's nondescript features functioned just as well outside Britain.

The next step was a visit to the Pension Walther in Schwabing. Wormser, cursing Schrempp for involving him, had to admit that he had given a room to the tall Englishman.

'Why didn't he sign the register?' demanded the detectives.

Wormser gave a cringing shrug. 'It was his first night, Officer. He was very tired after his long journey – I thought I'd not bother him till the morning. But he didn't come back.'

'Come and open his room – let's have a look at his luggage.'

Wormser was in a spot again. He had already acquired the case, when he had to restore the original owner's belongings in the room he had given to Draper. He tried to explain and tied himself up in a worse knot. Eventually he produced the case from his office.

'When he didn't come back I thought he'd ducked off without paying his bill … so I kept his case as security.'

The inspector had his own ideas about Wormser but the other matter was the more urgent. He rummaged through the case.

'No passport … no papers,' he said in disgust. In fact, Conrad's passport was floating in the North Sea, after Jacobs had flushed the pieces down the toilet of a B.E.A. Comet on his way back from Hamburg.

A junior detective picked up a silk shirt from the case. 'Made in London, sir ... has the initials C.D. on the neckband.'

'Corps Diplomatique?' suggested the inspector sarcastically. 'Come on, Wormser, you've been up to something ... tell me about the man who brought him here.'

'I didn't know his name ... I don't even know the name of this man.' He pointed to the case.

'Hard luck. Why did they come here – to this particular hotel? You must have known the second person.'

'I recognised him ... he stayed here once. He was an English student,' lied Wormser desperately.

Exasperated, the inspector grabbed Wormser by the arm. 'Come on, back to headquarters. Bring that case, Hans.'

When they arrived at the office, there was a list from the French Railways sent via Interpol. It showed that only twenty four males had booked all the way from Ostend to Munich at that slack winter period. There was only one name with the initials 'C.D.' and that was Conrad Draper. There was no address given.

'Have to check with London's Scotland Yard for that, they can get the full bookings from the London railway offices.'

'What about the other man?' asked his assistant.

'He was on the same train.'

Wormser came in for another heavy session of interrogation, but he gave a deliberately vague description that would have fitted a quarter of the population of Europe.

The inspector reported to his senior early next morning.

'I feel that both these men had only a fleeting association with Munich, sir. I think that the motives are all back in England and I suggest that we inform the London police of all the facts'

His chief, already flooded with local crime, was only too ready to give his blessing for the inspector to pass the ball to Scotland Yard.

Back in his office, the detective picked up his telephone and asked for London.

Benbow took the call about noon on the Tuesday. He rapidly noted down all the information, asked for written confirmation and, after profuse thanks, put the phone down. He dialled Information Room to find out why the case had been given to him.

'The officer who liaises with Interpol told us to put it through to you, sir.'

He rang the chief inspector concerned and was told something that almost sent him up to the ceiling.

A few moments later Bray came in with a fresh armful of papers.

'So! Here's a turn-up for the book, lad!' The Admiral was leaning back in his chair with a great grin on his face.

Bray waited patiently for the oracle to speak.

'Just had Germany on the blower,' announced Benbow.

Bray tried to imagine the Russian premier saying it in quite that tone of voice.

'Munich to be exact. They had a shooting there yesterday.'

The sergeant waited expectantly.

'Conrad Draper had a hole blown through his chest.'

Benbow looked so pleased with himself that Bray felt sorry when he had to say, 'Draper? Never heard of him.'

The Admiral's pale brows came together in a frown.

'Course you have, boy. The turf wizard of Brewer Street.'

Bray's face opened up slightly.

'Oh, him! Yes, I've heard of that chap. But what the devil's that got to do with us? Surely we've got enough on our plate already.'

He waved despairingly at the piles of documents littering the small room. Benbow sighed with the resigned air of a dedicated teacher of backward children.

'Listen, while uncle tells you all about it. This might be a tie-in with the Rita Laskey job ... and God knows we could do with one.'

He hoisted his feet up on to the corner of his desk and Bray sank on to the only other chair.

'I had this call from the German coppers to the effect that one Conrad Draper, of London, had been fished out of some bloody river there with a bullet hole in his chest ... in fact he was found in the water less than twenty-four hours after he had arrived by train from England. Part two of the mystery ... another bloke who was with him just before he was knocked off, was on the train with him – and he's vanished.'

Bray looked blankly across the desk.

'So what? Why drag us into it?'

Benbow's fat lips gave a Cheshire Cat smile.

'That's what I wondered when Morris rang me – the Interpol Liaison bloke. I asked him why he'd shipped the call onto me, the most overworked and downtrodden character in the Yard. Know what he said? Calm as you like!'

Bray shook his head dutifully.

'He said that earlier this morning the Jerries rang up asking for a check on bookings on the train to identify this Draper and on the serial number of the gun that shot him. And stone me, it was a .25 Webley that was registered in the name of Ray Silver of the Nineties Club.'

It was Bray's turn to look surprised. He leaned forwards with his hands braced on his knees, as if he was ready to take off in a sprint.

'Silver and Munich. I don't get it.'

Benbow began destroying a pencil in his teeth.

'Nor do I. How the hell Conrad Draper fits into this, I

just don't know. But here's another thing. The German post-mortem says that he had injection marks on his arms. Looks as if the common factor running through this case is drugs, chum.'

'But where does Golding – and the girl Laskey – come into this?'

Benbow shrugged.

'There's one thing similar – the bloke on the train and our friend Golding both have the knack of appearing and vanishing into thin air – could they be one and the same?'

Bray whistled. 'Nice theory – but we've only got the Nineties Club to link them up.'

The chief inspector hauled himself upright and reached for his Nikita-type felt hat.

'Yes, lad, theorising never bought the baby a new dress – let's get around to the Soho sin market and have a few words with the Draper outfit.'

They took a car to Brewer Street and climbed to the headquarters of the late bookie's gambling empire. Benbow enquired of the first clerk he saw and was directed to the big room at the front. From the attitude of the staff, the news of Draper's death had not reached them yet.

They found Irish O'Keefe making the most of Draper's absence. He was sitting behind the big desk, with a glass of Conrad's whisky in his hand and one of his cigars stuck in his lips. Another half-dozen lay safely in his pocket.

He leaped up guiltily as Benbow pushed his way into the room. Irish scowled when he saw it was the police and dropped back into his seat.

'What's the game? We don't like coppers coming here – it's bad for business.'

Benbow sat on the corner of the desk, snatched the cigar from the little man's mouth and glared down at him.

'Here's some news that's going to be even worse for business. Conrad Draper is dead ... murdered.'

Irish turned white on the spot.

'You wouldn't be after kidding me!' he croaked.

The detective shook his head slowly.

'Come on, Irish. Let's hear your end of the story. I haven't had the chance of dragging you into the nick since that last bit of false pretences you pulled – but I'm always ready for another trip.'

It was an empty threat but O'Keefe was too shaken a man to realise it. He gulped, took another swig of his late boss's whisky and talked.

'He belted off the day afore yesterday – got me to book a train ticket and sleeper to Munich … was it there he was done in, Mr Benbow, sir?'

'Yep, shot with a gun from the Nineties Club.' Irish's eyes almost popped out on to his cheeks with surprise.

'Not Silver's! But he took it off him.'

His voice trailed away as he realised that he might be saying too much. In his philosophy, half a word was too much to tell a copper.

Benbow leant over and grabbed his shoulder.

'So you know something about it, eh? Look, chum, I'm not in the mood to mess around with you. You spill it now, or I promise I'll take you in as an accessory after the fact and throw the bleeding book at you.'

He put such virulence into the words that Irish, with the knowledge that his boss and protector was no longer available, decided to cough.

'He was like a mad thing on Friday night, sir … he went around the Nineties Club very late and Silver must have told him then that Golding was going to Munich next day' His voice died away as Benbow and Bray closed around him to stare at him as if he was the Oracle of Delphi. He looked up at them fearfully.

'Sure, I only said the truth, sir,' he began uneasily.'

'You're doing fine … carry on,' said Benbow exultantly. Bit by bit the whole story, as Irish knew it, was unfolded. How Conrad had been cuckolding Golding, the business of the tape recorder, the attacks Draper had made on Silver, and how he had taken the Webley from him.

'Why did he go to Munich after Golding?' demanded Benbow.

'I don't know at all, sir … Draper wasn't the sort of man you asked. He told you if he felt in the mood, but if he didn't he was just as like to knock your block off – powerful big man he was.'

He shook his head sorrowfully and took another suck of spirits. 'Don't know what we're going to do now, I don't.'

'What d'you know about Golding?' snapped Bray.

'Nothing about him, if you know what I mean. I'd seen him in the club, I knew he was keeping Rita … but what he did, I don't know.'

'Come off it, Irish,' grated Benbow. 'Your boss was tramping the same set of stairs to the Laskey woman … you must know something about him … why did Draper go after him to Munich?'

Benbow had at last found a small chink in the solid wall of non-cooperation in Soho and was determined to lever it wide open.

'Draper was as mad as hell when he heard that she'd been croaked – he reckoned Golding had done it.'

'Why should Golding have done it … just because he'd found that Conrad was sleeping with her?'

Irish shrugged nervously. 'Search me, guv'nor.'

'Did he ever threaten Golding?'

Irish considered this over another swig of Scotch. 'He never had a chance … he had me on the runaround for days trying to find Golding.'

'And did you?'

'Sure, never a wisp of bleeding hair did I see!'

'And what colour was his bleeding hair?'

Bray could almost see the mental brakes going on as the shock of Draper's death began to fade and his natural distrust of the police take its place.

'I don't remember – sure, that was just a figure of speech.'

Benbow, who was now standing alongside the little fellow's chair, grabbed it and tilted it back. Irish went back with it, spilled his drink into his lap, and howled as Benbow slammed the chair back onto an even keel.

'Listen, O'Keefe, cut that out. I know you've been Draper's watchdog for years. But your boss is dead now and if you don't help me nail his killer, I'll rake up enough dirt on you to keep you inside for a twelve-month. Now come on, let's have some sense. You know damn well what Golding looks like – and where he comes from.'

He finished his speech with a resounding thump on the back of the chair which jerked Irish forwards.

'I only seen him a couple of times, honest,' he whined. 'He was the sort of bloke that don't look like anybody in particular.'

'How tall was he … fat, thin, dark, blonde … come on.'

O'Keefe gave a convincingly genuine but utterly useless description of Golding. Benbow scowled.

'The average man again! Irish, if you can't tell us what he looked like, tell me where he came from, what he did, where he went.'

The ugly dwarf from Dublin made routine protests again but eventually told what he knew.

'The only place I ever saw him was the club. He didn't know me nor Conrad. He used to take Rita there … I heard he was pretty thick with Ray Silver.'

He hesitated and looked from one to the other.

Benbow caught the look and bent down so that his bulbous nose was almost pressed against Irish's face.

'Spill it all, sonny – it may save you a short haircut and a heap of mail bags.'

Irish gulped and took the plunge.

'Conrad was on the hook – not much, no mainlining,

only skin-pops – but he used to get his junk from Ray Silver ... and I heard tell – not Gospel, mind you – that Golding was the big man with the supplies. He used to distribute to all the hundred-deck men.'

'And this gun was the one that Conrad took from Ray Silver?'

'Yes ... Conrad never used an iron.'

Benbow kept at the little man unmercifully but eventually was satisfied that he knew no more of any importance.

'Take him down to the Division and get a statement, Bray,' he said at last. 'Don't charge him with anything yet until we make up our minds which offence will get him the longest stretch.'

He threw a baleful glance at O'Keefe and strutted to the door as if he were about to take the salute in Red Square.

At the Yard, he found that the sergeant from the Drug Squad had left him a report from the laboratory. This confirmed that the white powder from the shelves of the safe was a mixture of morphine and heroin. There was also a long cable from Germany giving the details of the post-mortem and investigations on the body from the River Isar.

When Bray came back about four o'clock, he found Benbow thoughtfully staring at the dusty picture of the 1936 water-polo team, which was the only ornament in their office.

'The plot thickens, lad. We've had the report from Munich, with a photo ... it's certainly Draper. And the lab have found drugs in that dust from Silver's safe. So with O'Keefe's evidence, we've got enough to take him in. The Nineties Club should be out of business for a few years.'

Bray looked puzzled. 'Why did all this business happen in Munich? If they wanted a punch-up, they could have done it here just as well. And where the hell is this Golding now?'

Benbow tapped the transcript from the laboratory.

'This is the answer in Munich. It's one of the places on the Near East pipeline for narcotics. Vienna, Paris and the Balkans are the big places, but Munich is a clearing house as well. It gets in from Turkey and the Levant as well as directly from the Far East.'

'You think they went there to collect the stuff?'

'I'm sure Golding did ... don't know about Draper. We've no evidence to say he ever dabbled in the business side of dope, only the pleasure aspect, if you can call it that.'

Bray wandered restlessly around the room.

'What do we do now? All this seems so disjointed. Bits and pieces of crimes with Golding's name running through it all. What are we dealing with: a homicidal maniac or a dope smuggler?'

Benbow shrugged magnificently. 'Search me, comrade, but we're going round to see this Eurasian creep. He may be able to throw some light on it – before we drag him off to a cell. He'll be one less fly on the Soho dung heap. Give Sergeant Roberts a buzz, will you. I promised to let him know.'

Again the club was visited at a discreetly early hour. This time it didn't matter, as Benbow had authority to close the club as being undesirable premises pending Silver's prosecution. He arrived with the two sergeants at about six thirty and barged past the astonished doorman, who was rigged out in a pullover instead of his Victorian outfit.

The three detectives marched through the deserted club, past the chairs piled high on the tables and the empty bar. A single bare bulb burned in the ceiling and no one, not even the barman, was in sight.

'Hope the bastard is here,' muttered Benbow as they filed through the alleyway backstage to Silver's office.

They found him standing at his cupboard, counting

bottles of spirits. He swung round in surprise and gave a crafty grin when he saw who had arrived.

'What d'you want this time, coppers?'

Benbow wasted no time or words but strode across the room and put a detaining hand on the surprised owner's arm.

'Ray Silver, I am arresting you and you will be duly charged with being in unlawful possession of narcotic drugs, namely heroin and morphine, in contravention of the Dangerous Drugs Act. Anything you say may be taken down and used in evidence. Now then, chum, what d'you say to that?'

Silver's face came up in red blotches that matched the red brocade waistcoat that stretched over his spherical stomach. He shook Benbow off and went to sit behind his desk, clawing his way like a blind man along the edge.

'What are you trying to pull this time?' he asked huskily. 'I want my lawyer – you know damn well there's nothing here, you looked the other day.'

His voice was shaky and hardly more than a whisper.

'We found enough in your safe to fix you, Silver,' said Sergeant Roberts harshly. He had a hatred, amounting almost to an obsession, of drug traffickers. He had seen too much of the degrading results of their trade to show any sympathy when they were caught.

Benbow was less emotional about it. He grinned at Silver's deflation.

'You want to use stronger boxes next time – the last ones leaked.'

'I want my solicitor,' blubbered Silver. He reached out a shaking hand to the telephone.

Benbow calmly trod on the loop of flex that hung over the end of the desk and the instrument came crashing down to the floor before Silver could touch it.

'Oops! Sorry, accidents will happen,' grinned the Admiral, leaving the phone lying dismembered on the carpet.

'Look, chum, you're for the high jump but if you cooperate with us a bit, we might put a word in for you before the judge puts on the Black Cap.'

Silver wavered then plumped for the chance to get his sentence reduced. He told them the whole story, ending with Golding's trip to Munich.

'He went out of here like a bat from hell – raving mad!
'

'And he took your gun with him?'

'Yes – a .25 Webley – I had it legally too. Police permit, licence – the lot!' countered Silver defensively.

Bray took Silver away to the West End Central Station to be charged, while Roberts and Benbow stayed behind to have another look around the club. They went to the deserted bar and turned the lights on. Between them they went through the place with even more enthusiasm than the time before. All the shelves and cupboards were turned out, but nothing came to light. Benbow looked in a recess under the sink and saw a waste bin. Something odd struck him but it was a few seconds before he could pin it down.

'Roberts – come and have a shufti at this.'

The sergeant came over and looked.

'Cellophane paper – looks like lots of cigarette wrappers.'

Roberts looked at the packets under the big mirrors and nodded.

'All wrapped as usual.'

Benbow stared at the cellophane in his fingers.

'I've seen a gag like this with gaspers before,' he mused. 'Are there any more in the cupboards?'

Roberts went back to another shelf behind a glass door, in the comer of the bar.

They found what they wanted here. A couple of dozen uncrushable packs had had their outer wrappers stripped off. Between the cardboard and the silver paper inside was a thin polythene envelope, filled with white powder. Benbow rubbed his hands delightedly.

'Lovely – just what the magistrate ordered, eh, Roberts?'

They carefully wrapped up the rest of the cigarette packets and went down to the police station.

Bray had just finished taking a statement from Ray Silver. The Eurasian was sitting dejectedly behind a cup of cold police station tea in an interview room.

'Silver, we've found enough heroin in cigarette packets in your dump to send you down for years. What have you got to say about that?'

Silver had plenty to say, most of it unprintable, but the gist of his words was to the effect that it must belong to someone else. 'Where did you find it?' he demanded.

Benbow told him and he poured out another torrent of foul language.

'That effing Snigger, that's who you want,' he squealed. 'The cunning bastard. Look, I take back all that statement. It was Gigal that was behind this … done it all behind my back and got the blame put on to me.'

He gladly gave them Snigger's address in South London. Now that he suspected Snigger of splitting on him, Silver was all for dropping his employee as deeply into the mire as possible. By eight o'clock, Silver was locked in a cell, and the Nineties Club had been padlocked by the police.

The detectives went back to the Yard and Benbow and Bray tramped up to their box-like office to turn to the next problem, the tracing of 'Snigger' Gigal.

'Shall I get the Division to pick him up in Fulham?' asked Bray, his serious sixth-form face anxiously reflecting his eagerness to get on with the chase.

Benbow picked up an appetising new pencil and eyed it thoughtfully.

'I wonder?' he mused. 'Will he run now that he knows

we're on to the drugs angle? He might lead us to Golding if we're lucky. Let's give him a bit of rope.'

He lumbered to his feet and pushed his hat to the back of his head.

'Take Sutcliffe with you ... watch Gigal for the next few hours and see if he goes anywhere that might be a lead to Golding. If he hasn't tried to communicate before midnight, you'd better knock him off and we'll try to get something out of him.'

Benbow's hunch came off. Half an hour later, Bray was sitting in a coffee bar almost opposite the Nineties Club. He had a clear view of Gerrard Street and of Detective Constable Sutcliffe, who was leaning against the wall of the pin-table saloon next to the club. Sutcliffe looked eminently in character, with sideboards, a thin moustache, and pointed shoes.

At twenty to nine, a small man walked briskly up to the club door then stopped and looked in puzzlement at the new padlock. The spiv-like character levered himself off the wall and came over to him. 'No good trying to get in, mate – they closed it up just now.'

'Who did it?' he said, pointing uneasily at the padlock.

'The rozzers, mate – they hawked the boss man off in irons too.'

Sutcliffe was a devoted amateur actor and he warmed to his role now.

'Are you a member?' he hissed dramatically, 'because if you are, I'd chuck my card away and buzz off before the bobbies come back.'

Snigger muttered under his breath, looked furtively up and down the street, and hurried away to the pub on the comer in search of more details.

Sutcliffe gave a discreet thumbs-up sign to Bray, who left the cafe and followed Snigger into the public house.

Across the crowded smoke-filled bar, he saw Gigal

talking earnestly with the landlord and being told with expressive pantomime what had happened at the Nineties Club that evening. Snigger downed a double whisky then hurried out to hail a taxi.

By this time, Sutcliffe had brought the police car from further down the street and had parked it near the public house. It was an unobtrusive blue Morris Oxford, a borrowed 'Q' car, instead of the usual black Wolseley which would have given the game away. They were able to follow the taxi through the slow traffic without any trouble.

'He's going in the opposite direction to his home,' observed Sutcliffe. 'He lives down in Fulham.'

They were now heading up the Tottenham Court Road.

'Are we to tail him wherever he goes?' asked Sutcliffe, with visions of all North London and the country beyond in front of him.

Bray shrugged. 'Let's see what happens – he's turning right here anyway.'

The taxi stopped near the University Union and the barman got out.

'Drive straight past and stop around the next comer,' snapped Bray. Before the constable had brought the Morris to a stop, Bray was out and walking back to the comer. He sauntered after Snigger and followed him a short distance to the block of flats in Ferber Street.

He hung about when the ex-jockey went inside. As soon as he heard the slam of lift gates, he dodged into the open entrance hall. The automatic lift had a row of lights above the door and he waited until the red flicker stopped at the fourth floor. A moment later, Sutcliffe joined him and they both stood concealed in the stairwell.

Before long, the lift motors whined again and as Snigger stepped unsuspectingly into the hall, they moved forward and hustled him off to the Yard for questioning.

Chapter Thirteen

Paul Jacobs might have found it difficult to explain why he walked past the block of flats and carried on without a pause to the end of the square. Something intangible triggered off his outsize sense of caution. He crossed the road and walked past his hideout without so much as giving the building a second glance.

It was three days after Snigger's visit and the square was in its mid-afternoon peaceful period. The slight young man with long side-whiskers who leant against the railings around the dusty patch of grass looked nothing like a policeman, even to Jacobs. Probably there were fifty such loungers at that moment in London, all reading their newspapers and minding their own business.

But a second after seeing him, Paul looked up at the fourth-floor windows and saw that his bathroom curtains were not hanging exactly true. He may have left them like that, he thought, but it was unlikely. He was a man of obsessive tidiness, both in his business and criminal ventures and in his personal ways. He suddenly felt convinced that someone had been into the flat since he was last there – and he had no caretaker or cleaning woman.

He crossed the road and walked within a few inches of the waiting man, who took not the slightest notice of him. Reaching the corner of the square, Jacobs doubled back along the lane behind Byng Place and approached the flats from the rear.

As he passed the opening of a mews, he saw a police car concealed in a garage entrance. At the back of the flats, where the boiler house was placed, he saw a young and athletic-looking street cleaner leaning on a brush in the centre of an already perfectly swept lane.

Paul's razor-edge sense of self-preservation reared on its hind legs and he went rapidly back to Goodge Street Tube station and found a telephone box. He dialled the number of his flat and waited. There was a long pause and, for a time, he thought that there would be no answer. Then the ringing tone clicked off and a voice said gruffly, 'Hello, who's that?'

He made no reply but put his receiver down and quickly made his way down to the platform to catch a train to Paddington and the safe obscurity of South Wales.

In the flat, Benbow stood rattling the button of the telephone. Then he dialled the operator and got through to a supervisor.

'Chief Inspector Benbow here, miss, any luck with that call?'

'Sorry, sir … it was far too short. All we can tell you is that it came from a public callbox in this exchange area.'

He grunted his thanks and dropped the telephone back into its cradle.

'Three bleeding days, and then when we do get a call they can't trace it,' he complained to Bray, who was busy slitting open cushions with a penknife.

'Don't suppose it matters – if he's as cunning as he has been up till now we wouldn't catch him with a hoary old gag like that.'

Benbow nodded gloomily. 'That's if it was him – he didn't say a word.'

They had paid three previous visits to the flat since Bray had found it and had a man in there ever since, hoping to catch Golding when he returned.

On entering the place on the Monday evening, they had found a note from Gigal pushed under the door. It was addressed to 'Mr G.' and read:

156

'ALL UP THIS END. SOMEBODY HAS SQUEALED. MAYBE SILVER, THOUGH HE'S BEEN NICKED AND THE CLUB CLOSED. BE VERY CAREFUL. THE BUSIES ARE ON TO YOU. I AM SHOVING OFF TONIGHT BEFORE THEY PICK ME UP. USE THE STEPNEY ADDRESS IF YOU WANT TO GET IN TOUCH BUT I'M KEEPING LOW FOR A COUPLE OF MONTHS.'

Snigger had been denied the chance to shove off, but had steadfastly refused to say anything at all about Golding. In spite of all Benbow's efforts, he refused to say anything except to repeat that he was innocent of any charge that was brought against him.

He showed considerable sense in doing this, thought Benbow with ungracious admiration. The clever crooks who say nothing usually get off better than those who unburden themselves with the mental purge of a long confession.

After Gigal had been remanded, the detectives, including Turnbull from the laboratory, came back to the flat. They turned it inside out in the hope of finding something that would help to trace the elusive drug smuggler and murderer. There were a few clothes in the wardrobe but all were good ready-mades from London stores. There were fingerprints in plenty that matched those in the Newman Street flat, but this put them no further forward.

'Not even confirmation that he killed Draper,' moaned Bray. The butt of the Webley that had been sent back from Munich showed a confused mixture of prints. Although it had been under the waters of the Isar, it still carried some blurred dabs, but these matched Ray Silver and Conrad Draper only.

'Not surprising,' commented Bray. 'Everyone, especially murderers, would be wearing damn great gloves in December'

The only hope that the laboratory people had been able to offer was that of identifying contact traces from the clothing. Using a miniature vacuum cleaner, which sucked air on to a minute disk of filter material, they collected a quantity of reddish-grey dust from the turn-ups of one of the pairs of trousers that Golding had left behind.

'What's this – some other exotic drug?' asked Benbow when Turnbull showed him the filter pad.

'No. I haven't a clue ... some of it seems a bit metallic. The boys will let you know as soon as they've done a micro and spectography on it.'

True to his word, the liaison officer brought him a report on the Friday morning, the same day that Golding shied away from the flat in Bloomsbury.

'The dust turned out to be a very finely divided mixture of silver, copper, and nickel,' said Turnbull.

Benbow stared blankly at him. 'Why the reddish colour?'

'That was iron oxide dust ... better known as jeweller's rouge, Archie.'

The Admiral grabbed the form and waved it over his head in mock exultation.

'Oh joy! And what the hell does all that add up to? Is he a chemist or a metallurgist or something?'

Turnbull waited patiently for Benbow's bout of exhibitionism to pass off.

'Looks as if friend Golding has some connection with a place where metal plate is polished – you know, dishes and cutlery. The dust is all either silver itself or copper or nickel, both used as a base for silver plating. Copper was the base for expensive Sheffield plate, but nickel is used now for the cheaper stuff.'

Benbow whistled through his false teeth. 'He might be in the jewellery or antique trade, you think?'

Turnbull shrugged. 'That's up to you – but he's

certainly been standing somewhere where a lot of metal polishing has been carried out – what conclusions you draw from it is your affair.'

'Was it a lot of dust?'

'I'd say it was certainly more that would come from a few casual cleanings of the household trophies ... of course, he might collect the stuff for a hobby, but even so, the amount we got from his turn-ups was more than a gram – suggests work on almost a commercial scale.'

Bray, hovering in the background, threw in one of his customary wet blankets. 'An uncle of mine always has the stuff over his trousers – he's dotty on old silver, but that's only a hobby – he's a bank manager.'

Benbow scowled at him.

'Got any better ideas, sonny? – cause if not, we'll get down the flat again and see if there's anything we missed the first twice.'

In the afternoon, they went back to Ferber Street again and went up to Golding's flat, where a plainclothes man had been on duty ever since they had tracked Snigger to the place. The chief inspector sent the watcher down to keep an eye on the entrance while he and Bray set about searching the rooms for the third time. With the help of Sutcliffe, they went through all the drawers again, examined the furniture for hidden spaces and pulled up all the fitted carpets once more.

The phone rang while they were making a last desperate attack on the cushions and chair seams.

Benbow turned after the phone episode was over and surveyed the chaos in the lounge. In spite of the wrecked appearance, the only actual damage was to the velvet-covered cushions.

'We can give up the watch on the place now,' he said gloomily. 'Golding will be off his lair like a dose of salts after that call – and God knows which end of Britain he'll hide out in.'

Bray turned to the last chair, a leatherette easy chair with the same brown cushions as the others. He slid his hand down the crack at the side and felt all around.

'Here's something … oh hell – a threepenny stamp – big deal!'

He slapped it in disgust onto the mantelpiece and carried on with his destruction of the cushions.

Benbow mooched around the flat again and came back to watch his sergeant finish the job.

'Sutcliffe has been fishing around in the bathroom – had the lino up and looked down the waste pipes – no joy though.'

'What are we supposed to be looking for anyway?' complained Bray.

'I'll tell you when we find it,' said Benbow snappily. The frustration of getting a little bit further and then meeting a brick wall was irritating him more and more as the days went by.

Bray's fingers felt all along the remaining cracks and into the wadding of the cushion. 'Damn all!' he said disgustedly.

Benbow turned away and idly picked up the stamp in his hands.

'Looks quite new – not even creased,' he said with a yawn. Then his brows drew together in sudden concentration. 'Bray – look at this!'

The sergeant took the stamp, turned it over in his fingers and looked questioningly at his chief.

'Just an unused threepenny stamp – looks new, as you say – but I can't see what earthly use it is to us.'

'Can't you? You try going out of here and buying a stamp like that.'

His voice was suddenly full of bounces and eagerness. Bray stared at the stamp for a few more seconds before the penny dropped.

'A dragon? A ruddy dragon!' he exclaimed.

Benbow beamed like a fond father.

'That's it, lad – you can only buy those in Wales.'

Back at the Yard, they took the stamp to the lab on the upper floors of the New Building and got someone to make sure that there was nothing extraordinary about the stamp apart from its place of origin.

In his office, Benbow sent for a trade telephone directory for the South Wales area and riffled through the pages eagerly.

'Why South Wales?' Bray made his inevitable objection. 'There's a North as well, they sell the same stamps there.'

'Because two-thirds of the population live in the south – we've got to start in the most likely places.'

'And what if some visitor to Golding's flat happened to drop the stamp? Golding himself still might come from Kent or Westmorland – or even Golders Green!'

Benbow groaned.

'I'm going to get rid of you, Bray. You get on my bleeding wick … talk about a regular Doubting Thomas. Look, if you don't make a shot in the dark now and then, you'll never get to be a rich chief inspector like me, chum.'

He found the pages listing jewellers, antique dealers, and silversmiths. There were less than a score of antique dealers, but well over a hundred jewellers. The Admiral groaned when he saw the list.

'We'd take a month of Sundays to go through those – let's have a crack at the antiques boys first.'

'You can exclude any big shops, combines, and chain store jewellers,' observed Bray, losing some of his pessimism, 'Golding would almost certainly be working on his own to be able to go flitting around like he does.'

His chief nodded over the directory. 'Sure – we can narrow it down to a man with his own business, probably – if there is any business at all, that is.'

'And we know he's not a very young man or a really old josser – nor has he got one leg or a hunchback,' added Bray facetiously.

'He's somewhere in his forties, according to the miserable descriptions we've had so far,' agreed Benbow.

He riffled through the pages of the yellow book again.

'And he's not very tall, very short, cross-eyed, bearded or bandy, so we want an average-looking bloke of middle age, who runs a silver business and often goes to London for a few days.'

His sergeant's face suggested that he thought this was Alice in Wonderland stuff, but he managed to keep his tongue still.

Benbow started by phoning the C.I.D. chiefs of the six police forces in the counties of Glamorgan and Monmouthshire. He explained what he wanted and asked for their cooperation. This was readily given, though some of the Welsh detectives were politely incredulous.

Benbow confirmed and amplified his requests by Telex to each of the police headquarters, then went home to bed.

The weekend was quiet, nothing being heard from any of the Welsh constabularies.

On the Monday morning, a report from the Newport, Glamorgan County and Merthyr Tydfil forces said that there was no one on the list of dealers who at all resembled Golding in appearance or habits.

In the afternoon, there was a false alarm from the Swansea police force. They thought they had found a jeweller and silversmith who was nondescript enough to be the wanted man and who frequently spent long weekends away from home. But an hour later, a crestfallen detective inspector rang through to say that a tactful series of enquiries had given the man a cast-iron alibi in the shape of an attractive schoolmistress in Gloucester.

The afternoon wore on and Benbow began to feel the

accusative eyes of Bray saying, 'I told you so,' following him around the little offices. He began to wonder if he had better widen the net to take in the dealers in West and Mid-Wales, but at five o'clock the miracle came across the wires.

'Cardiff City here … Detective Inspector Parry. We've raised a likely candidate for you, seems to fit the bill very well … name of Paul Jacobs. But the chief says to go very careful on this one. If it's a load of bull he doesn't want any comeback, thank you very much!'

Bray and Benbow caught the eight o'clock train from Paddington to Wales. The Admiral was bouncing and beaming and his sergeant openly sceptical as the diesel rumbled out of London for the long run westwards.

Chapter Fourteen

'That big house on the end – the one with the double garage.' Parry, the Cardiff detective, pointed out a large modern villa set amongst trees in a select suburban avenue of the Welsh capital.

With Benbow and Bray, he sat in a police car – a Vauxhall this time – which was parked a respectable distance down the road from Paul Jacobs' home.

'He's not in now, is he?' asked Bray in a worried voice. He had developed a very healthy respect for Golding's knack of smelling trouble at a distance.

A plainclothes constable in the front seat reassured him. 'No, I've been watching since half past eight – he went out about nine.'

Parry explained how they had been keeping tabs on Jacobs since the day before.

'Edwards here has been tapping the odd-jobber who does Jacobs' garden ... that was it, wasn't it, Edwards?'

The junior detective nodded. 'He likes to knock off for a fag and a gossip every now and then, so I was able to pump him quite easily.'

'Have you ever seen this Paul Jacobs, Inspector?' asked Benbow.

'No, if he's your man, I thought it unwise to let him get wind of me ... according to you he's as slippery as the original greasy pole.'

'You can say that again,' said Archie, with feeling.

Inspector Parry shook his head in wonder. 'I still can't credit it. This man is well known in city business circles – couldn't have a better reputation. He's even in the same golf club as the chief constable.'

Bray grinned at his boss behind the local officer's back as Parry leaned forward to speak to the driver.

'Turn round and go back to Llandaff nick, Thomas.' He turned to the London men.

'No point in staying in sight more than we need.'

As they moved off through the pleasant suburb, he enlarged on the bare facts he had given them before.

'This chap, Jacobs, is about forty-five to forty-eight – that right, Edwards?' The man in front nodded.

'He's got an antique shop down near the docks – a small place, just a bit of silver in the window. I've asked the local division about it. They say they've never heard anything at all from there – no break-ins or suspicion of stolen property finding its way there. He's got an oldish man who looks after the shop. Jacobs does all the buying, that's why he's away so much.'

Benbow interrupted. 'Is it a genuine business or just a front, d'you think?'

Parry was emphatic. 'Oh, genuine, no doubt of that – I've made a few enquiries and plenty of people have dealt with him.'

Edwards added to this, 'He only handles good stuff – all silver. He never advertises, he goes on dealers' recommendations and that. It's a genuine set-up all right, sir.'

Bray looked over his shoulder at the affluent residential area they were crossing. 'Would a poky little shop like that turn in enough money to keep up a house like his?'

Parry shrugged. 'I've never seen a poor jeweller yet.'

'What about his trips away?' asked Benbow rather impatiently.

'It's been difficult to find out actual dates without putting him on his guard,' replied Edwards.

He was a bright, chirpy young man. Benbow thought that he was cut out to get to the top in record time.

'We know he goes away about ten days in every month,' put in Parry. 'Usually every fortnight but not absolutely regular. We had a policewoman snooping around the local shopping centre yesterday – she found out that Mrs Jacobs varies her shopping lists according to whether he's home or not.'

'What's the wife like?'

'Very nice by all accounts. Quiet, pleasant, in her middle thirties, I think – perhaps a bit older.'

'He definitely went away last Thursday,' cut in Edwards. 'The gardener said that he came home unexpectedly the next day – the wife wasn't expecting him, sent the old man out next morning for a loaf.'

'You seem to have got plenty out of the gardener,' observed Benbow.

Edwards grinned. 'Any gardener – even at seven-and-six an hour – will talk about anything under the sun if it gives him a chance to lean on his spade instead of using it.'

They were approaching the local police station now, not far from the famous cathedral. In the charge room, Parry spoke aloud the thought that was passing through all their minds.

'Well, is it him, or isn't it? How are you going to decide?'

Benbow, missing his pencils, chewed his knuckles instead.

'Two things would clinch it – either his fingerprints … God knows we've got enough of those to compare – or get Irish or Gigal to identify him.'

'Gigal wouldn't do it … O'Keefe might.'

Benbow gnawed away at his fingers.

'No hope of getting anything out of the house with his dabs on, I suppose?'

Parry shook his head. 'Don't see how we can … illegal and it would put the wind up him straight away, if he's the

167

chap.'

'What about the shop?' suggested Bray. 'There should be plenty there carrying his prints – all that polished metal stuff.'

Edwards had a flash of inspiration. 'Take something in for valuation – I could do it. He'd have to handle it and give it back, wouldn't he?'

Parry and Benbow mulled it over and agreed it was the simplest way.

'But you'd better not take it, Edwards. You've been hanging around the house too much,' objected Parry.

'What about Sergeant Bray here? He's a complete stranger.'

Bray was all enthusiasm. 'If you could get me something right now, I could do it this morning. We've brought a photograph of Golding's prints from the Yard.' He rummaged in his briefcase and took out a standard identification form with copies of the dabs from both London flats that Golding had occupied. Bray's keenness was infective – the local men put their heads together and in a moment Parry thought of something suitable.

'My sister's teapot! She had a good one given her for a wedding anniversary last month. It would do fine, as we'll have to offer Jacobs something genuine or he may smell a rat.'

'Can you get it?' asked Benbow.

'Yes, I think so,' said Parry optimistically. 'I can talk her into lending it to me for a couple of hours ... it can't come to any harm, can it?'

Around noon, a police car pulled into a side turning off Bute Street in Cardiff's dockland.

The notorious Tiger Bay area, now respectable with its new high-rise flats, lay quietly under a pale winter sun as Bray clambered out of the Vauxhall, clutching a cardboard box with reverent care.

Parry leaned out after him and pointed down the street.

'Second on the left … and for God's sake look after the ruddy thing – there'll be another murder if anything happens to it.'

The sergeant took an even firmer grip on the boxed-up teapot and set off down the road. He passed a line of empty condemned tenements, then turned a corner and made his way towards James Street, a busy road reminiscent of the days when this was the busiest port in the world. Before he reached it, he came to a small shop with steel grilles set behind the window panes. Above the brown painted door was the simple legend *Paul Jacobs – Antique Silver*.

With a sudden intuitive feeling that this was the end of the search, he pushed the door open. The interior had been partitioned off so that there was only a small cubicle inside the entrance, with a counter facing the door. An inner door with two Yale locks was set in the high wooden partition to his left.

Bray stood clutching his box, wondering whether to rap on the green baize counter for attention. Then silently an elderly man appeared behind the counter. He had half-moon spectacles on his nose and wore a grey linen shop-coat.

'Can I do anything for you?' His voice matched his mild and rather remote manner.

'I'd like this teapot valued, please.'

Bray lifted the top off the box and pushed back the tissue paper to reveal the glistening bloom of solid silver.

The old man nodded slowly. 'Do you want to leave it?'

Bray shook his head.

'No, I've had an offer for it today and I wanted to make sure that I wasn't being robbed – if you get me,' he ended lamely.

He had prepared this patter but now, in front of the calm old assistant, it seemed to fall flat on its face.

The man in the grey coat seemed incurious.

'It'll take a few minutes. Will you wait, please?'

He began to shuffle off with the box and Bray gabbled at him.

'It will be Mr Jacobs himself who will look at it? I've had such good reports of his valuations – I'd like him to do it.'

The other looked at him mildly over the tops of his lenses. 'Certainly, if that's what you want. Just wait.'

He glided away, leaving Bray with the impression that he moved on small wheels instead of feet. Bray prepared himself for a long wait but within a couple of minutes another person materialised from behind the partition.

In spite of the hard crust that Bray had grown after years in the Metropolitan Police, he felt a sudden tensing as he faced what might be a double murderer. He saw a man of average height, with a composed, smooth face, fair hair swept back over his forehead, and a small moustache – a new feature according to the scanty descriptions.

At that instant, Bray, the Doubting Thomas, the thorn in Benbow's intuitive side, felt that this was Golding. He suddenly found that Jacobs – or Golding – was speaking.

'… quite a nice piece. A pity that the handle has that tiny split, it stops it from being perfect. Still, if I were selling it, I'd ask about thirty-eight guineas.' He turned the elegant vessel around under the shaded light to admire it. 'Yes, say thirty-eight. If someone gave you forty for it, they wouldn't go far wrong.' He looked up, a faintly apologetic smile on his face. 'Of course, I couldn't give you quite that, if you intend selling it.'

Bray hurriedly reassured him, imagining Parry's face if he went back and told him that he'd sold his sister's anniversary pot.

Bray had seen with satisfaction that the dealer had left good fingerprints on the silver. The sergeant had carefully polished it before he left the police station and had been careful only to handle it by the rim afterwards. Jacobs wrapped the teapot up and handed it back across the counter.

After paying the valuation fee, Bray left the shop feeling a little unreal. Not many detective sergeants could have paid seven-and-six to a man they intended arresting for a capital offence, he thought as he walked back towards the police car. For now he was utterly convinced that Jacobs was Golding. He felt sure that checking the prints was going to be almost a formality and that within minutes they would be back to take him into custody.

He would have been less elated if he could have heard the conversation in the back room of the shop immediately after he left. As the door shut with a valedictory buzz, Jacobs went back to the office behind the partition. His old assistant turned from polishing plate, brushing reddish dust from the front of his coat.

'Funny business, that chap,' he said slowly. 'From London, by the sound of him ... wonder why he wanted that piece valued?'

Jacobs glanced idly at Ben. 'What's so odd about that? It's our job, isn't it?'

The old man stared pensively at the plate.

'I know that teapot ... it was only sold from Carter's up in the town about a month ago. I recognised the cracked handle. Why would he want it valued again – Carter's price is reliable enough?'

Jacobs' attention was caught now.

'Are you sure it was the same one, Ben?'

'Yes, not only the handle but there was a little dent on the base. I remember seeing it in their window.'

A tickle of suspicion began in Paul's mind, as the old assistant went on, 'I thought at first this London fellow might have stolen it but he insisted that I got you to look at it personally – he would hardly have done that if he'd pinched it.' Ben paused and scratched his head slowly.

'Didn't seem like a thief anyway – thought he had more the manner of a policeman.'

Paul Jacob had the same sensation that he had had when he walked past his flat in Ferber Street the week before – a sudden clanging of alarm bells in his brain, then a feeling of the ominous nearness of danger.

He turned abruptly to his safe in the corner. 'I've got to go home, Ben ... just remembered some papers that I need.'

The old man noticed him pulling out some papers and a bulky envelope which he stuffed rapidly into his briefcase. A moment later he was gone.

About half an hour after Bray had returned to the car with the sacred teapot, two police cars swept down the long, straight stretch of Bute Street, hurtling towards the antique shop. Parry and Bray were jubilant after their recent successful session in the fingerprint section of Headquarters, but Archie Benbow was strangely worried.

'Too damned easy for my liking. Find a bit of dust, then a threepenny stamp, a set of prints that match and bingo! Much too smooth, there's got to be a catch in it somewhere.'

There was a catch in it. When they got to the shop, their bird had flown.

Parry made the reluctant Ben shut up the shop and go with them.

'Said he was going home, did he?'

'Yes, to get some papers,' said Ben, mystified.

'Passport and money most likely – how the hell did he rumble us?'

They hurried to the cars and shot back to town, blue lights flashing and gongs going. Parry picked up the radio handset and contacted Information Room.

'Get a car to Oakdene Crescent – quickly. Intercept a grey Ford Zephyr belonging to Paul Jacobs of Number

Seven. I don't know the registration number yet.' Ben had told them the make and colour of the car but had no idea of the number.

The two cars raced towards Llandaff, but on the way Benbow dropped Edwards at the main railway station with instructions to watch the barriers for Jacobs.

While they sped across the city, Parry spent most of the time at the radio. He called for a rapid search at the Taxation offices for the registration number of Jacobs' car and put out a general call to adjoining forces for them to pick the Zephyr up at sight – as soon as it could be identified.

A third patrol car joined them as they reached Llandaff and when they screeched around the comer into Oakdene Crescent, they found yet another black Vauxhall parked outside Jacobs' house. Benbow hopped out and ran to it. The driver, who had answered the first radio call, waved towards the house.

'He's gone, sir, the car's not in the garage.'

Parry, Bray, and the Admiral hurried up to the front door, leaving the other uniformed men to spread around the back of the property. Before they could ring the bell, the door flew open and an indignant woman in an apron erupted onto the porch to demand to know what was going on.

'Are you Mrs Jacobs?' asked Benbow harshly.

A voice from inside the hallway answered over her shoulder.

'No, I am! What are those men doing in the garden? Who are you?'

Parry rapidly introduced himself and the Yard man.

'Where is your husband, Mrs Jacobs? Has he been here this morning, within the last few minutes, I mean?'

Mrs Jacobs, her usual calmness shattered, looked in consternation from one to the other. 'He's only been gone a few moments – what on earth do you want with him?'

173

'I'm sorry, Mrs Jacobs, we need to question him very urgently in connection with some serious criminal charges.' Benbow, in the middle of his urgency, found time to change his voice to a gentle tone. 'It's most urgent, I assure you.'

Barbara Jacobs complicated the tense moment by dropping in a dead faint on the floor of the hall. Her daily woman, made of sterner stuff, glared at the detectives and dropped to her knees alongside the other woman.

'Now see what you done!' she hissed.

'Do you know where Mr Jacobs went? Did he take the car?' Parry rattled the questions off.

'He came home about a quarter of an hour ago – took some papers from his study and drove off – said he was in a hurry – dunno where he went.'

Parry swung round to Edwards, who had just trotted up the drive.

'Stay here with the wife – take her down to the station as soon as she's fit. Before that, whip through the house to make sure he isn't still in there somewhere.'

With Benbow lumbering at his heels, he ran back to the patrol car and grabbed the microphone through the window.

'Information Room, got that Zephyr number yet? Hell, tell them to take their finger out. Keep that general call out, inform Monmouthshire as well – he'll probably try to get back towards London … yes, Paul Jacobs, wanted for murder … fair hair brushed back, average height. May possibly be armed. We're coming back to Central now.'

Before they arrived at police headquarters in the centre of the city, a call came through to say that the registration number had been traced and broadcast to all cars.

They had just entered the C.I.D. office, when the phone rang and Information Room told Parry that the car had been found parked and unoccupied off City Road. As they rushed back down to the waiting cars, Parry panted over his shoulder at Benbow, 'I don't get it – why stop in the town? I'd have laid bets on his making either for the London road or trying to get a train.'

They clambered into the car and shot off.

'This City Road – any significance in that?' asked Benbow, mopping his forehead with a handkerchief.

Parry turned from the radio for a moment.

'It's the motor trade area of Cardiff – dozens of showrooms and second-hand places.'

'What the hell can he want there – he wouldn't have time to buy a car, surely?'

'What about hiring a car – could he do that in this City Road?' suggested Bray.

Parry slapped his hands. 'Of course – hiring a car – there's umpteen of those places over there. Pay your money and drive away – no questions asked.'

He reached for the radio again.

'Relay to all cars free to join search in City Road area – check all car-hire firms for man answering description taking car in last thirty minutes – get details of vehicle if found … treat as most urgent.'

Their own car tore across the city and reached the street in record time. They parked alongside two other patrol cars which were hemming in a grey Ford Zephyr.

Uniformed police were already flitting in and out of the brightly-lit showrooms that lined the half-mile of City Road, enquiring about the recent renting of a car.

'Could take ages – even if our theory is right,' groaned Parry. 'There must be a couple of dozen places that rent cars, some of them in the side streets – a lot of garages do this hiring racket.'

Bray looked at the abandoned Ford.

'A clever so-and-so like Golding might have left this thing as far as possible from his intended destination, just to fool us.'

In fact, Jacobs had not had time to go very far, but he

had hopped on to a trolley bus and gone a mile from where he had left his Zephyr before finding a car-hire firm in a quiet backstreet.

He rented a modest black Morris Minor from the proprietor. The man had no reason to be interested in him, but to cover his tracks as much as possible, he had combed his hair to one side while in the trolley bus and pulled on a plastic raincoat and a ratting cap which he always carried in his car.

With an assumed stoop, he looked a different man as he paid in cash for the car, signed some fictitious name and address, and drove sedately away.

He went in the opposite direction to London, his ultimate goal. Forty minutes later, while twenty of the Cardiff police force were frantically searching the City Road motor shops, Jacobs drove into Bridgend, a country town twenty miles to the West.

He parked his Morris in the furthest corner of a public car park and walked to the railway station, swinging a small case containing a few hundred pounds in cash and two of his false passports.

There was a fifty minute wait at the station before the next London express came in and he had a niggling fear that the Morris might be spotted, if luck was against him. But it was an hour after the train left before Parry's men found the place where he had hired the car and another six hours before a local constable spotted its number plate in the Bridgend car park.

By this time, Jacobs was in London. With his usual caution, he had locked himself in the toilet when the train stopped at Cardiff and, in case Paddington was being watched, he left the train at Reading and caught a bus the rest of the way. While the detectives in South Wales were fuming over his repeated vanishing trick, he was booking in at a small hotel in Victoria.

He had a good meal and went to bed to consider his

next move. It was only too clear that this was the end of an era for him. He had lost heavily. He was down but not beaten. Drawing on his peculiar divided personality, he was able to look on the loss of his home, his wife, and a way of life with dispassionate regret. There was certainly regret. He was very fond of Barbara – it seemed unlikely that he would ever see her again. She had had no inkling of his other life and he sincerely regretted the trouble that she would be drawn into now that the truth was out.

Yet in the middle of this disaster, the greatest since the Nazi war machine had collapsed and thrown him adrift, he was already plotting for the future. He had to get out of Britain – that was the first necessity. Once abroad, he could set about rebuilding his empire. He had thousands of pounds salted away in various banks on the continent and he knew many contacts who would help him return to the drug trade.

Before he turned over to sleep, he comforted himself with the thought that there would be more Ritas and Elsas on the continent. There might not be another Barbara, but he'd had a good run these last fifteen years.

Paul Jacobs, alias Golding, alias Schrempp, was far from beaten.

Chapter Fifteen

'We've lost him for good now,' said Benbow dejectedly. Four days after Paul Jacobs' getaway from Cardiff, he and his sergeant sat dolefully in their office at the Yard and admitted defeat.

'The swine may be sitting half a mile away this very minute,' said Bray. 'It's fantastic really – we know who he is and we can't pick him up.'

'That Identikit picture you had in the papers and on the telly … how good was it?' asked Roberts.

Benbow looked at Bray, the only one who had ever seen Golding. He shrugged non-committally.

'I don't know. Each feature on its own was correct – nose, eyes, chin, you know. But all put together – well, it just wasn't him. Could have been anyone, let's face it.'

Benbow's hand stole towards his pencil tray. 'If only – we'd had just one photograph,' he said, 'There wasn't one bleeding snap in the whole house – he must have been canny enough to look ahead just for a situation like this.'

There was a thoughtful silence, broken only by the splintering of timber as the Admiral made a meal of another HB.

Bray sighed heavily. The youngest of the group, he was itching for action. He was ready to dash outside and begin taking London apart brick by brick until he found Jacobs.

'Any ideas, anybody?' said Benbow.

'What d'you think he'll do?' asked Roberts. 'Run for the continent or stick it out here?'

'He's got to live,' replied Benbow. 'He'll probably have a stack of money on him, but he can't get any more from his normal account under the Jacobs name. I should think he'd try to get back to the continent – he may already have done it.'

They were interrupted by the phone. Benbow answered it and within seconds, a great smile cracked his round face. He jabbered a string of thanks down the phone and delicately dropped it back into its cradle.

'That's something to help box the swine in the country, if he's still here – Parry, the D.I. from Cardiff, rang to say he's found a photo of Jacobs. He's teleprinting it up right away and sending the original by post … Bray, as soon as it comes, get it out to the Press Officer for newspapers and the telly, and get it on handbills.'

He rubbed his hands energetically.

'This'll give Mr Bloody Jacobs something to worry about.'

It did make Paul Jacobs worry, but it also helped him to make up his mind about his next move.

He first saw the photograph of himself blazoned across the Saturday evening papers. A very good likeness of himself stared out of the front page, with 'HAVE YOU SEEN THIS MAN?' printed in heavy capitals across the top.

The dailies had been carrying a story on the Draper murder on and off for a few days, and when the Yard let drop the escape of their prime suspect from their trap in Cardiff, the more sensational national papers had really made a meal of it. There were articles every day speculating on the whereabouts of the man who could assist the police in their inquiries and now the gratis offer of a photograph from the Yard was like manna from Heaven to Fleet Street.

Paul Jacobs stuffed the paper in his pocket, pulled his hat down a trifle and hurried back to his hotel. He packed quickly and left for Euston, where he used his left-luggage ticket to get out the American-style hat and coat. With these on and a pair of rimless glasses, he felt a little easier, especially as he already had his moustache well grown.

Sitting in the refreshment room, he looked again at the offending photograph. It was a large blow-up of a group picture and he cursed the Cardiff golf club under his breath. Though he habitually shied away from the camera, he remembered that about four years before he was unable to avoid being included in a group that had won a local championship match. He lightly cursed his friend, whoever he might be, who had public-spiritedly offered the picture to the police, but then he philosophically accepted the damage that had been done.

It decided his course of action – he must leave the country at once. The faint hope that he might fade away into London and start under a new identity was now far too risky. Any fool with the price of a newspaper might point him out to a policeman in the next week, day or even hour.

He must get abroad – and quickly. It was get out and stay out this time.

Jacobs left the restaurant and caught the tube to Whitechapel, then a bus to Poplar, near the India Docks. He found a small boarding house on the road to Millwall in the heart of Dockland. It was a cut above the usual seamen's lodgings and catered mainly for the less exalted ship's officers.

In the sitting room, he found the current issue of *Lloyd's List* and looked up the German ships expected in the Port of London. He was looking for any one of several vessels, ships that he had used for his smuggling. The paper told him that the motor vessel *Rudolf Haider* was due on the Monday evening.

The master of this ship was an old friend of his, as ruthless and hard as Jacobs himself. He was well aware of Jacobs' smuggling and had shared in the profits more than once. In fact, it was the *Rudolf* that had brought over the last consignment from Hamburg, concealed in tent frames.

Paul settled down to a couple of days waiting at Millwall. He registered in the boarding house as a Swedish fourth officer waiting for his ship. It was easy to avoid any contacts with the other guests and the Scottish landlord was a dour, incurious man who left him well alone.

He spent the weekend either in his room or at the cinema. On Monday morning, he ventured up to the City to close an account in another name, which gave him a further five hundred pounds in cash which he changed to Deutschmarks at another bank.

Jacobs learned that the *Rudolf Haider* was coming into Surrey Commercial Docks with timber and was due to sail for Bremen on the Thursday morning with a cargo of machinery.

Late in the afternoon, he bought a dark hair-rinse at a chemist's near Aldgate and went back to his lodgings. He paid his bill and left Millwall, then went to a public wash-and-brush-up establishment near the Blackwall Tunnel. Here, in the privacy of yet another of the cubicles that had seen so much of Jacobs' double life, he quickly dyed his hair in the wash-basin and darkened his eyebrows. Putting his hat on the still damp hair, he walked out past the sleepy attendant looking even less like his photograph than ever.

Crossing the river to Bermondsey, he found similar lodgings for the night. He kept out of sight for most of the following day but, as dusk fell, he began his final sprint towards his Fatherland and comparative freedom.

The mid-December night fell with a chill drizzle. About six thirty, he caught a bus and got off near the main entrance to the Surrey Commercial Docks in Lower Road. The Transport Commission policeman on the gate made no effort to challenge him, but Jacobs crossed to the little lodge and enquired in Germanic broken English the way to the *Rudolf Haider*.

The officer obligingly pointed down into the distant

swirl of lights and fog.

'*Rudolf Haider* ... Albion Dock, berth four. Down there, mate, turn left.' He fumbled for a German word. 'Albion Dock – left – *links*, see ... der schiffist in Albion Dock ... er, berth fier ... savvy, Fritz?'

Paul hurried through the wet darkness, under lonely electric bulbs fixed to wooden poles, tripping over railway lines laid across the roads, until he came to the dockside. Great stacks of timber lay everywhere, and at the water's edge, a line of immobile cranes stood like rusty giraffes.

He stumbled on, gripping his case, until he came to a row of gaunt warehouses. On the ship moored alongside the first, he saw the name *Rudolf Haider – Bremen* painted across her stem.

She was a modem tramp, not the rusty tub of pre-war adventure stories. A sleek motor-ship, she was neat and fast, equipped with all the latest devices for touting around Europe for cargoes. The cargo of pine and spruce from the Baltic had been partly unloaded and the decks stood high above the quayside. A steep gangway stretched from the deserted dockside up to her midships companionway.

Paul hesitated for a moment in the shadow of a warehouse then strode boldly up, his shabby suitcase banging awkwardly against the stanchions. In spite of the deserted appearance from the quayside, a man on watch appeared as he reached the ship's side. He was a grizzled old fellow in a blue jumper and a beret, leaning over the rail at the top of the gangway. He took a pipe from his lips, spat into the oily water twenty feet below and challenged Jacobs in broken English.

'You want see somebody, huh?'

Paul's manner suddenly changed. His shoulders went back, he seemed to get taller and even the fibre case in his hand suddenly seemed to get more respectable.

'Tell your captain that I have arrived,' he said in crisp autocratic German. It was the voice of a Prussian autocrat, not that of a down-at-heel seaman. The watchman responded at once to the authority in the tone. He jerked upright and threw a hand towards his beret.

'Ja, mein Herr – zvieheisensie, bitte' he asked respectfully.

'Schulman – Franz Schulman.' He used the name which was on the passport he travelled on from Munich last time.

The sailor hurried forward and Paul followed him more leisurely. He passed several lighted portholes, the clink of glasses and loud laughter coming from one. Beyond these, the deck was deserted. A few lights gleamed from behind thick glasses screwed to the bulkheads, but the whole effect was dank, chilly, and eerie. The dockside looked like a graveyard and the ship smelt of wet wood and diesel oil.

The watchman's boots clattered up a ladder ahead of him and Jacobs followed up to the boat deck. A row of doors faced him as well as the dark aperture of an open companionway. The man had vanished and Paul stood uncertainly, waiting in the gloom. Then the nearest door burst open and a short, fat figure stood silhouetted in the bright opening.

The captain came forwards with hand outstretched.

'Schulman ... what are you doing here?' He had a harsh voice, but it had a welcome note of sincerity.

Jacobs turned his face so that the direct light from the cabin did not fall on it. The old seaman was standing alongside the captain and Jacobs made a significant nod towards him. Herzog swung around and dismissed the man back to his watch with a few curt words.

'Come in – come in,' he said to Paul, with a curious look at his suitcase. 'Here to stay, eh?'

The captain led the way into his cabin and soon Jacobs was settled with a glass of Swedish schnapps. He explained to Herzog that he was on the run from the

184

British police and wanted to get back to Germany on the *Rudolf*. He said nothing about the murder charges, but said that he was wanted for the narcotic offences. Herzog was not particular about mere dope smuggling but Paul knew that he might shy away from being involved with abetting a murderer, especially when one of them took place in Germany itself.

'So I've got to clear out back to the old country, Otto – make a fresh start and work up the trade back there. I've got all my suppliers intact in Munich and contacts in Brussels and Marseilles. I can't touch England for a few years – too risky. Perhaps I'll try the States when I've worked up some more capital.'

The mention of money brought a gleam to Herzog's eyes. 'It's a great risk taking you back, Franz ... we're going to be lying here for another day and a half ... then there's the Bremen immigration to deal with. I'm the only one to help you – my officers these days are too damned honest.'

Paul saw only too well what he was driving at and slid a hand into his side pocket. He dropped a thin wad of West German banknotes onto the table in front of the captain.

'There's fifteen hundred marks – I'll give you another fifteen hundred in any bar you care to name – as long as it's in Bremen ... outside the dock gates!'

Herzog slowly picked up the notes and flicked through them thoughtfully.

'It's not much – considering the risk.'

Paul gestured his inability to do better.

'It's all I've got.'

Herzog shrugged resignedly. 'OK – but only for old time's sake. You'll have to keep out of the way. Most of this crew is new, I can't pull the wool over their eyes as I did with the old lot.'

They talked for an hour, Paul weaving some satisfactory story to account for his flight from the British police. He hoped Herzog would not come to learn the truth about the murder before the ship reached Bremen. There was no television aboard and the captain read little English by choice, sticking to cargo manifests rather than newspapers.

'Where can I stay,' he asked Herzog, after a lot of talk and too much schnapps.

The captain rubbed his chin. Like the rest of his face and his whole body, it was round and pink. He looked at Paul from his little black eyes. 'I can't actually hide you now – that watchman has seen you and he's as loose-mouthed as a hungry python.'

He saw Jacobs' worried frown and reassured him.

'It'll work out. You'll have to be a relative of mine getting a cheap trip home. I'll put the word around at breakfast, before that garrulous old swine on watch makes a mystery out of it.'

'Where can I sleep?'

'There's a spare cabin down at the after end of the boat deck accommodation.' Otto thumbed vaguely over his shoulder. 'Kept for a fourth officer when we have one.'

'What about eating?'

'Yes, a problem. We don't want you too prominent, there are shore people hanging around all the time we are in port.'

'I could be ill – probably will be once we leave dock,' he added with a touch of grim humour.

Herzog took him down a passage that crossed from side to side of the boat deck, between the cabins. At right angles to this was a second passage which formed a T with the first, running fore and aft.

He was given a small cabin at the after end on the port side. A steward brought some bed linen, made up the bunk, then brought a tray of supper. Jacobs lay on the bunk, looking as listless and ill as he could manage, though he cleared the tray of food. The steward, a stolid

Westphalian, took little notice of him.

Herzog looked in late at night.

'Everything all right?'

'Yes, as long as you don't ask any Scotland Yard men on board.'

'You're on German soil now.'

Jacobs avoided telling him that after the affair on the Brudermühlbrücke, that was not the slightest consolation to him. The Captain left and Jacobs slept until the noise of cranes and winches woke him next morning.

It was still dark, but unloading was going on by the lights fixed in the rigging of the *Rudolf*. When the steward came again with breakfast, Paul muttered something about influenza coming on. Without a word the man left and came back with half a bottle of brandy and a box of aspirins.

The day dragged and he sat thinking about his wife, for a long time. His affection for her was deep and genuine, quite different from the steel-like casing around his moral sense when it came to murder, mistresses, and drug running. Already, plans formed vaguely for reunion with Barbara at some place abroad. Once in Germany, he intended writing to her, getting someone like Herzog to mail the letter in Britain.

But all this was in the future.

Shaking off these nebulous schemes, he left his bunk and went to the porthole. It was late afternoon and the rain had cleared off. He stared through the thick glass at a red watery sun as it reached the cranes on the far side of the Albion Dock. For a few moments, his face was lit up by the orange glare, framed in the circle of the porthole.

Outside on the boat deck, a passing officer glanced up. He saw the face shining in the glare of the setting sun – and almost fell on the deck with shock.

Radio Officer Adolf Busch sat in his cabin two doors away

from the passenger and pressed the bell for the steward. He had just thrown back a double gin but was still white about the face.

Baumann, the morose steward, tapped the door and came in. He stood mutely waiting for orders. The radio operator rarely called from his cabin. Busch said nothing, just sat there with an empty glass in his fingers, staring at the writing table before him.

'Ja?' prompted the steward.

Busch jerked his head up. He looked ill – sick to death.

'Baumann … who is that man in the spare cabin?'

The radio officer was looking at Baumann's face, but his eyes were looking right through him to a vision twenty years old.

'You know his name?' he asked tonelessly.

'Herr Schulman, the captain called him – Franz Schulman.'

The radio man made no reply, and the steward got restless.

'Anything you want?'

Suddenly Busch came to life. He jumped up and grasped the older man by the shoulder.

'You take him his meals, Baumann,' he gabbled feverishly, 'I want to see him close up – the next meal, give me your jacket. I'll take the tray to him.'

The steward, shaken out of his usual impassiveness, drew back from Busch and goggled at him as if he'd gone berserk.

'Why … what are you doing?'

The radio operator calmed himself with an effort.

'Look, don't worry … just tell me when his next meal is due. Why don't he eat in the saloon with the rest of us?'

'He's sick. Got a bad chill. He eats well enough though. I'm due to take him his supper at six thirty.'

'I'll take it – call in here with the tray.'

The steward reluctantly agreed and left for his pantry.

Busch sat for a long time on his bunk, his face set and drawn. He stared at the opposite bulkhead, his mind far away in space and time.

The radio operator spent the night without a wink of sleep. After his brief visit to the cabin along the passage, he was a mental wreck. The long night passed with agonising slowness, his clock seeming more like a calendar.

At six in the morning, he could stand it no longer. It was the day they were due to sail – the previous evening, the ship had shifted her berth to the Pool of London to take on a few tons of special cargo. She was going back to Germany very light this trip. The small consignment of machinery would be swung aboard in the London River during the morning and by afternoon she would be battened down and ready to sail on the evening tide.

Busch had no duties until then and by eight thirty, he was washed, shaved, and in his best uniform. He caught a taxi and by nine o'clock was waiting on the steps of the West German Embassy in the West End.

At four fifteen that afternoon, a distinguished member of the Diplomatic Corps of the Federal German Republic was ushered into the presence of Superintendent Gleeson at New Scotland Yard.

Gleeson was one of the Special Branch officers and his particular pigeon was liaising with the Aliens Department – keeping tabs on the members of other nations whose presence in Britain was suspect.

Gleeson, another large calm man of the type that abounds in the senior ranks of the British police forces, rose to greet his top-brass visitor.

He shook hands and pulled out a chair.

'A pleasure to meet you again, Herr von Grauber. How can I help you this time?'

Von Grauber, a caricaturist's dream of a Prussian

aristocrat, sat down gracefully and spoke in English conspicuous only by its perfection.

'I think perhaps it may be the other way round, Superintendent – it is a matter of considerable urgency, so I shall not waste words.' He opened an elegant briefcase and took out a thin folder. 'This morning, the radio operator of a West German vessel berthed in London came to see me.' He opened the file and glanced at the top sheet. 'This man was very agitated and frightened. The crux of the matter was this. The previous evening he caught a glimpse of a man being given a passage back to Germany on this ship. He thought he recognised him and, by a pretext, managed to get a closer look. I should say that the conditions under which this passenger is housed seem furtive, to say the least. The radio man was convinced, by this second look, that the mystery man was a former SS officer wanted in Germany for certain war crimes.'

He turned over another page in the folder.

'This ship's officer, Busch, was a signals corporal in the Wehrmacht in nineteen-forty-five. The battalion to which he was attached had a most gruelling time at the front during the Allied invasion and was withdrawn only in time to save the whole morale from crumbling. The day following their return from the front, there was a major Allied offensive on the Rhine and they were ordered back into battle. They went to pieces completely and though they did not get to the point of actual mutiny, a detachment of SS was sent to deal with them.'

The Prussian's face was set and hard. He was talking of this to one of the enemy, however far in the past it had happened.

'The details are best forgotten, but the outcome was that more than twenty soldiers were shot and many more dealt with in a barbaric fashion. The SS colonel responsible was tried at Nuremburg and hanged. Other officers were also punished, but one, Oberleutenant

Schrempp, was never traced.'

He paused for a moment

'Last night, this ex-corporal Busch recognised Schrempp as the man hidden on board the vessel *Rudolf Haider* in your Surrey Docks.'

Gleeson nodded politely, but still wondered where all this was getting them. He had a hell of a lot of work to do and he had had his fill of the German Army in the Western Desert many years ago.

Von Grauber went on before the detective could intervene. 'The ship sails in a few hours. To make sure that we were not making fools of ourselves, the Embassy phoned the War Crimes Commission in Frankfurt this morning and got them to wire a photograph and the main points from his dossier.'

The German paused to give his punchline its best effect.

He swivelled the folder around to Gleeson and flipped a page over so that a photograph of a face was presented to the Yard man's view.

'That is the man ... the radio officer confirmed it ... and I think many thousands of people in Britain would recognise him as well.'

Gleeson stared blankly at the photo. In his specialised branch he had little contact with ordinary crime, but then the penny dropped.

'Good God! That's the chap they've been flashing over the TV and papers – the Cardiff killer!'

He looked up in amazement at von Grauber. The implications were startling enough to shake even his impassive nature. The Embassy man smiled with modest pride and saluted with a Prussian jerk of his head.

'I thought it might interest you – as far as I remember from newspaper reports, this man is wanted for serious crimes both here and in Bavaria.'

Gleeson was already reaching for his phone.

'I think our need for him is greater than yours, Herr von Grauber … hello, get me Chief Inspector Benbow, please.'

Within minutes, Archie Benbow had joined them, having hurled his rotund body along the corridors of the Yard at a speed never equalled since he left the beat. Gleeson rapidly got him up to date and showed him the photograph of Golding. The Admiral beamed and rubbed his podgy hands together.

'Bloody marvellous – this character is as full of tricks as a cartful of monkeys … but with a bit of luck, we've got him now.'

He turned to von Grauber. 'I'm afraid, sir, that we'd like first crack at him if we're going to catch the beggar. We want him for two murders and a long string of narcotics offences. I don't know if we can get him hanged on it – it was murder with a firearm, capital murder under the fifty-seven Act – but it was done abroad … what d'you think, Superintendent?'

Gleeson shrugged. 'I don't know, Archie … he's committed two murders on separate occasions – that's a capital offence, as well, unless the one abroad doesn't count.'

Benbow's smile persisted.

'In any case, Herr von Grauber, we'll get a life sentence at very least – then we'll turn him over to your people for hanging!'

The German looked pointedly at his wristwatch.

'I suggest that unless you do something quite soon, neither of us will have the opportunity. The ship moved from the Surrey Commercial Docks to the Pool of London on this morning's tide to finish loading and is due to sail for Bremen on this evening's tide … it is now four-forty-five.'

Benbow stood up quickly. 'What time is high water?'

Gleeson reached to a shelf behind him and picked up a newspaper. He crackled the pages with agonising slowness until he found what he wanted.

'London Bridge – six-twenty-two. Another hour and three quarters.'

Benbow was halfway to the door.

'I'm on my way … don't want to cut it too fine.'

He rushed back to his office and sent Bray for a car and a couple of detective constables. He rang Information Room and asked for the assistance of a patrol car, which was to meet him at Billingsgate.

Within a few minutes, Archie Benbow was crammed into a black Wolseley with the three other detectives and a driver, swearing their way slowly through the rush hour traffic.

The driver did his best down the Embankment but, even with the gong ringing, they made very poor time to Blackfriars. As they sat fretting in a solid jam at the end of the bridge, Benbow leaned forward and tapped the driver on the shoulder.

'Knock off the bell and the flasher when we get into Lower Thames Street – we don't want to scare the pants off this chap … he's given us the slip too often in the past.'

As an afterthought, he prodded the other man in the front seat.

'Call Information Room … tell them to find out from the P.L.A. where the ship is berthed in the Pool. And tell them to buzz the other patrol car to make sure that they don't go clanging their way up to the gang plank.'

Cursing the one-way systems, the driver squeezed his way up Queen Victoria Street, Cannon Street, and eventually reached Lower Thames Street, which runs along the upper side of the Pool of London, the highest reach of the river which can be used by big vessels through Tower Bridge.

'Better stop here … the other car should be around the comer,' commanded Benbow. This was the territory of the

City Police Force, independent of the Metropolitan, but in a case like this, there was no argument about priorities.

They nosed into a side turning and saw the cranes and warehouses of the Pool a few yards ahead. It was now twenty-past-five. The offices were turning out and the pavements were crowded with people hurrying to buses and tubes.

Benbow and Bray got out into the dusk and walked to the quayside. They stood under a crane and looked out at the mass of lights that was the Pool and the opposite bank of the river. There were three ships moored out in midstream, lit like Christmas trees, and many more lined the banks of the river.

Benbow glared in frustration at the confusing array of vessels.

'This is bleeding useless ... let's get back to the radio and stir the Yard up – they should have contacted the P.L.A. by now.'

They hurried back to the car and the driver contacted the Information Room again. They stood grouped around the nearside window waiting for a reply. Passers-by gave them curious stares and a couple of inevitable busybodies loafed around waiting for something to happen.

The other patrol car glided up and parked behind them, the mobile men in their soft hats and leggings coming up to join their group at the window. In a few moments, the message came crackling through the static.

'Green-Alpha-Four ... re your message of seventeen twenty-seven. Port of London Authority contacted as requested ... advised motor vessel *Rudolf Haider* sailed from Pool at sixteen forty-five ... repeat sixteen forty-five.'

Chapter Sixteen

'A quarter to bloody five … she just couldn't have!'

Benbow stood on the kerb and roared into the car, to the alarm of two young office girls passing at arm's length.

'Well she has,' answered Bray unhelpfully. He opened the door of the car and hopped in after the furious Benbow. The driver started the engine with a roar and then waited to be told where to go. The Admiral was pounding his thighs with bunched fists in sheer rage.

'An hour ago,' he snarled. 'If that Jacobs gets away this time, I'll hand in my cards, God help me if I don't. Driver, get going – down to Wapping River station. Use your gong, flasher, and flaming truncheon if it'll get you there any faster, but make it snappy.'

They all rolled back as the man let in his clutch with a jerk and accelerated into Lower Thames Street. Benbow clung on to the back of the seat and grabbed the microphone again.

'Information Room – Green-Alpha-Two – Chief Inspector Benbow. This is most urgent. Please contact Wapping – Thames Division – and ask them to have a boat standing by to take me down river. The *Rudolf Haider* must be stopped and boarded – murder suspect believed aboard. We should arrive at Wapping –' He broke off to look out desperately at the traffic. 'Some time today!'

Even with the best will in the world, a police car can never make good time through the City of London at twenty to six of an evening. It was ten minutes before they reached Tower Hill, lurching and swearing as the car swerved through the traffic, now up on the pavement,

195

sometimes careering along the wrong side of the street. Five more minutes went by before they reached the River Police Station.

The back of the peculiar building was a long landing stage, at which bobbed several little black launches flying the police pennant. The station inspector was waiting for them and Benbow explained the situation as they hurried down to a boat. The scene was lit by powerful floodlights and the dirty water looked an oily black by contrast. The night was not a cold one for mid-December, but there was a slight mist rolling up from the lower reaches of the river.

They clambered down into a launch, with Bray and the two detective constables close behind. A second launch was already swinging its bow downstream in front of them. With a roar of exhausts, their craft lifted up onto its bow wave and circled round to follow the other boat out into the dark, wide, river.

'I can't see how she got away so soon,' said Benbow. 'The tide wasn't full till six thirty.'

The River Inspector shouted above the noise of a ship's siren close by.

'I saw her going down an hour ago – she was very high in the water – she must only have had a part-cargo and ballast. Only drawing a few feet, I reckon, so she'd no need to wait for full flood to get out of the Pool – the tides are high this week.'

They had moved under the shelter of the open cockpit roof to avoid the cold spray thrown back as the little launch tore through the choppy water of mid-channel.

It was pitch dark now, just after six o'clock, but the river was a mass of lights. The south channel was full of ships preparing to run down to the sea and the other lane was jammed with strings of tugs and their barges taking advantage of the flood tide to get upstream.

'How far will she have got downriver,' shouted Benbow.

Inspector Price considered for a moment. 'What d'you think, Clark?' He spoke to the coxswain, a leathery sergeant with sailor written all over him.

'Hour and a quarter? With all this traffic about, she'll not do more than five knots – that'd put her somewhere past Greenwich.'

'Where will we catch her?'

'Cracking on Woolwich way, I should say, sir.'

They were overtaking a noisy tug and Price bent closer to speak to Benbow.

'Do you want us to radio Blackwall or Erith and get them to intercept her lower down? It'll take us all of half an hour to catch her in this boat?'

Benbow shook his head emphatically.

'No, there's nowhere else he can run to now – I hope!'

While the two little police launches forged on through the galaxy of lights on the misty river, the *Rudolf Haider* churned sedately ahead of them at quarter speed. Her radar spun around and picked out the innumerable hazards of the Thames ahead. In spite of the thin mist, visibility was good enough to see both banks.

From the high bridge, Otto Herzog and his Chief Officer stood with the pilot, watching the Thames unfold in front of them. They were following the stem lights of a Russian vessel, which was going too slowly for Herzog's taste.

The pilot, incongruously dressed in a City overcoat and a bowler hat, seemed quite happy with their progress and as they passed the Royal Naval College at Greenwich, Herzog walked to the north wing of the bridge to look at the opposite bank.

As he glanced astern, he noticed his passenger leaning over the rail of the boat deck. Jacobs – or Schulman as the captain knew him – was also looking astern at the receding lights of Central London. Herzog called down to him.

'Want to come up a bit higher?'

Jacobs climbed the ladder and joined the captain on the wing of the bridge.

'Glad to be seeing the last of it?' joked Herzog.

'I'll be happier when it's right down below the horizon,' said Jacobs with a touch of bitterness. 'And a damn sight happier still when I'm sitting in a Bremen taxi.'

He looked over his shoulder at a sudden noise, but it was only the second officer slamming the chartroom door.

'You'll be looking over your shoulder a lot from now on,' observed Otto, without much sympathy.

'I'll manage, once I'm back in the old country,' replied Paul.

He paused then a thought struck him.

'What's the idea of your radio operator acting as a temporary steward? I thought you liked a bit of style on your ships, Otto.'

The captain stared at him. 'What the hell are you talking about?'

His passenger explained. 'So when I saw him this afternoon in his smart uniform, I wondered what the devil he had been up to … pretending to be an assistant steward.'

Herzog frowned. 'Are you sure Busch did that?'

Paul nodded. 'Yes, he must be crazy.'

The ship's master shook his head sadly.

'And I thought he was supposed to be getting better, not worse … I'll have to keep my eye on him – poor chap.'

Paul looked curious. 'Why is he a poor chap?'

'He had a hard time in the war – broke him up for years. He's always been a bag of nerves, but never actually done anything as mad as this before … still, we can't blame him, I suppose. He was mixed up in some terrible affair with the SS once. He had to give evidence in the Nuremburg trials … never been the same since.'

An icy hand reached into Jacobs' chest and seized his heart. Suddenly, clearly, he remembered Busch. And with the memory, he knew why the man had tricked his way into his cabin. Safety, that elusive thing, slipped once more from Paul's grasp. He made one last effort to get a grip on it.

'It's cold, I think I'll go below,' he said abruptly and turned to clatter away down the ladder, leaving Herzog to stare after him from the bridge.

Jacobs hurried to the door of the radio room, which was next to the captain's quarters at the forward end of the boat deck accommodation. He stood outside for a moment and heard the crackle and bleep of radio apparatus which told him that Busch was inside. As he stood in the open cross-corridor, his mind raced, seeking an answer, like a cold, calculating computer.

Busch knew who he was – knew that he was the Schrempp wanted in Frankfurt for trial. A twenty-year-old phantom had caught up with him, one which was more dreadful than his recent crimes ... one which still carried the threat of the rope.

Busch could not have betrayed him yet, or else he would not be sailing down the river with him to the open sea. But Busch was the radio man – at any time in the next two days, he could turn a dial, touch a knob and tell Nord-Deutsche Marine Radio that the *Rudolf Haider* was bringing Paul Schrempp back to Germany.

Jacobs' brain ticked furiously, arranging facts like a computer. Busch, the queer silent one, the schizophrenic – the man tortured by memories so bad that he might be driven to take his own life.

It was dark and the Thames was deep and flowing fast. Jacobs slowly turned the door handle and pushed it open. He knew what must be done, and knew that it must be done quickly.

Busch was sitting with his back to the door, headphones clamped over his ears. His attention was fixed on the grey radio cabinets arrayed in front of him. Red lights glowed and needles jumped. On his left, a monitor from the bridge radar swept round and round, green streaks flaring up at every revolution to mark the position of nearby ships.

Jacobs walked softly to the back of the man's chair, his footsteps deadened by the headphones. He held his hands outstretched towards Busch's neck, ready to stifle the first cry.

Just before he reached him, the door slammed with a sudden gust of wind.

Busch started and turned around. His face froze in the most abject terror that Jacobs had ever seen. He half rose from his seat and his headphones fell off as Paul desperately dug his fingers into the man's throat. With the strength of sheer panic, Busch tore them away and promptly tripped over his chair. He fell flying back, landing flat on the floor. He made no sound, his mouth clamped tight by the fear.

Jacobs stood menacingly over him as he lay on the deck. Busch held a hand up partly in supplication, partly for protection. His attacker, briefly in the grip of an emotion as strong as the other's terror, forced himself to be calm.

'Who am I, Busch?' he hissed.

The haggard radio operator, intent on his own destruction, whispered, 'Schrempp,' then gave a piercing feminine scream.

Jacobs leapt at him. He lifted his shoulders and then swung the man's head back against the deck with a sickening crunch. Busch groaned and lay with his eyes staring, a dribble coming from the corner of his mouth.

There was a clatter of feet on the bridge ladder outside. Paul Jacobs flung himself to the door and slipped the lock across. A split second later, there was a hammering on the door and shouts in brusque German.

'Busch, Busch! What the devil is going on in there, Busch?'

Jacobs forced calmness on himself, willing his thudding heart to slow and his trembling muscles to keep still. He kept immobile behind the door while the shouts were repeated. After a few ineffectual rattlings at the door handle, he heard the feet hurrying back up the ladder.

He acted quickly, his ruthlessness coming to the rescue once more, especially now that his very life depended on it. Grabbing the inert body from the floor, he dragged it to the door and hoisted Busch over the threshold. As he strained with the dead weight, he calculated that if he could push the man overboard now, there was nothing to prove that Busch had not committed suicide. All the crew knew that the radio man was queer and over the last day or so, he had been acting even more oddly than usual. A splash in the dark and it would all be solved.

The radio room was directly astern of the captain's quarters, on the comer of the cross-arm of the T-shaped companionway. He was just going out of the radio room when he heard more loud gabbling from the bridge above.

Cursing, he lugged the radio operator's body around the comer and waited in the shadows. Immediately there was a clattering of several pairs of feet on the bridge ladder and he recognised the voices of the second officer and the captain.

Like a flash, he dragged Busch into the companionway, swung him up into his arms and fled around the comer into the central passageway. He reached the door of his own cabin and bundled the radio operator inside. There was nowhere else to go, so he leant against the inside of the door, panting and listening at the thick panels for sounds of pursuit.

As he waited, he suddenly felt the ship's engines begin

to pulse. He had not noticed them stop; they were certainly going when he had come down from the bridge a few minutes previously. He was in no state to be interested in the ship's navigation and he turned back to his own troubles, which were now coming thick and fast.

His eye caught a movement from the deck outside his porthole. The cabin was in darkness and the boat deck was lit quite well at that point by a bulkhead lantern. The movement crystallised into a group of men passing the porthole. As they moved through the yellow cone of light, Jacobs was horrified to see the wide stripes of a police sergeant's uniform on the nearest man.

Even worse, he recognised the fair young fellow in plain clothes as the man who had brought him the teapot in the Cardiff shop. These and several other purposeful-looking figures passed across his field of vision as they headed for the bridge.

The significance of the stopping of the engines now dawned on him, as he realised that the *Rudolf Haider* must have stopped to take the police aboard from a launch.

Blind panic possessed him for the first time in his life. The pressure of events had been too rapid and too harsh over the last few minutes. He tore open the cabin door and began to race up the companionway, intending to use the other side of the cross-passage and get onto the starboard side of the boat deck.

As he neared the junction, the sound of voices pulled him up short and shocked some sort of sense back into his brain. The words came all too clearly down the empty companionway ... indignant German mixed with the calm demands of the British police.

'... reason to believe that ... Paul Schrempp ... radio officer ... which cabin?'

The snatches of words wrought desperation in Paul Jacobs. He was cornered and knew that he was within seconds of arrest, with imprisonment and perhaps execution to follow. He twisted back down the central corridor to the extreme after end, where the narrow door lead onto the strip of deck looking over Number Three hatch.

As he fumbled with the handle, there was a bellow from behind. The Thames sergeant came around the comer and saw him from the far end of the passage. With the terror of pounding feet spurring him on, Jacobs got the door open and raced round to the starboard side beneath the boats.

He had no clear idea of what he was trying to achieve, but this was soon decided for him. From the cross-passage ahead of him erupted the figures of Benbow, Bray, and a river policeman. They headed for him and simultaneously he heard the approach of the sergeant from behind.

With the police only a few feet in front and behind he did the only possible thing. Running to the rail between the nearest lifeboat davits, he leapt up onto the wooden top and plunged feet first into the blackness of the Thames.

The iciness of the water was like an electric shock and Jacobs almost died there and then. But the wave of coldness passed into a numbing ache as the water closed over his head. With a suddenly clear and almost jubilant mind, he kicked himself back to the surface and began to swim.

For a moment he was too confused by the lights to know which way he was headed, but the steady gleam of the shore soon became clear and he struck out towards it in a powerful crawl. The cold passed off as his muscles drove his body into a fever of effort, but within a minute he had fresh troubles.

There was a double roar of engines as two police boats tore back around the stem of the *Rudolf Haider*. Directed by shouts from the ship's rail, they sped in a tight circle over her wake to the starboard side, combing the dark water with their searchlights.

One beam passed right over Jacobs in the first sweep, wavered and came back to fix in a glaring brilliancy. He dived and spluttered to the surface a few yards away. The light found him again and once more he had to go under. When he surfaced, the beam missed him but he saw that it would be only seconds before the two lights caught him again.

Desperate now, he struck out for the bank, still a hundred yards away. It was then that he saw the tug bearing down on him, towing a string of barges which shone dully in the wildly swinging searchlight beams.

The little vessel was almost level with him, going at a good speed down river with her long tow-rope just visible. She was very close and getting closer. As Paul swam towards shore the tug churned past, the wash from her propeller splashing over him as he thrashed through the cold water.

Already he had grasped the slight chance that the new arrival had offered. Putting on a spurt he lashed past her stern, right into the froth of the wake, trying to get between the tug and the first barge. Once on the other side, he would have a couple of minutes grace from the police launches, which were still in midstream.

Summoning up every last bit of strength, he tore in an Olympic-standard crawl to beat the approaching barge. The blunt nose loomed enormously over him in a matter of seconds and the bow wave actually caught him and threw him away from the rusty plates of the ugly vessel.

He had just made it – the swirling water took him round the nose on the side farthest from the searching beams of the launches.

His lungs bursting with effort, Paul stopped swimming and lifted his head out of the icy water to take stock of his position.

It was the last voluntary thing he was ever to do.

In the last second of his life, with the calmness of

inevitable death on him, he stared along the side of the barge into a steel funnel which meant oblivion for him.

There were two barges, side by side, and he was between them.

Their steel flanks met where the taper of the bows ended but, with the choppy water and the speed of the tug, they were moving apart and crashing together rhythmically as they bore down on him.

Paul Jacobs was carried on the bow wave into the gap. Like a giant nutcracker, with eighty tons on either jaw, the sides of the two barges slammed together, again and again as his body was washed along between them.

What came out at the other end was recovered the next day. It caused a wrinkle of disgust to appear even on the face of the hardened pathologist who examined it at Deptford Mortuary.

The loose ends of the case were stretched over half of Europe.

'More bleeding work than a dozen straight murders,' growled Benbow, a few days later. 'And not even the satisfaction of a pinch at the end of it.'

A contended Bray looked up from an avalanche of statements on his table.

'I don't know, we've got a few characters in the can ... Silver, Irish, Gigal ... the skipper of that ship. And that poor flaming radio operator has got a load off his mind.'

Benbow masticated a green pencil as he thought of the complications with the Federal German Republic. Their ship had been arrested, moored in the river and the captain charged with being an accessory to murder. He stoutly denied everything but, even if the Germans succeeded in getting him back for trial at home, he was unlikely to be seen on the high seas for a few years.

Benbow stared out of the window at his blank wall

opposite and absently champed on some splinters.

'Amazing bloke, that Jacobs or Golding or what the hell you like to call him,' he reflected. 'He'd have got off under our damn noses again if that Busch fellow hadn't spotted him. I wonder how his wife will get on. I feel sorry for her.'

Bray stared at the water polo team.

'Parry said on the phone that she thought it was for the best … but I don't know. It was a hell of a way to go, between those barges.'

Benbow picked timber from his tongue. 'Thank God that most of the villains around here haven't got his brains. If they were all like Golding, I'd give up the force tomorrow and go and raise chickens.'

Bray muttered inaudibly to his blotter, 'And the eggs wouldn't have the little lion – they'd have the Red Star!'

The Sixties Mysteries
by
Bernard Knight

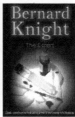

The Lately Deceased
The Thread of Evidence
Mistress Murder
Russian Roulette
Policeman's Progress
Tiger at Bay
The Expert

For more information about **Bernard Knight**

and other **Accent Press** titles

please visit

www.accentpress.co.uk

15162123R00127

Printed in Poland
by Amazon Fulfillment
Poland Sp. z o.o., Wrocław